TOUGH LOVE

THE SHAKEDOWN SERIES

ELIZABETH SAFLEUR

Elizabeth SaFleur LLC
PO Box 6395
Charlottesville, VA 22906
Elizabeth@ElizabethSaFleur.com
www.ElizabethSaFleur.com

Edited by Trenda Lundin
Proofread by Claire Milto
Cover design by LJ Designs

ISBN: 978-1-949076-25-7

1

Luna ran her fingertip along the envelope of the Valentine's Day card. It was silly, really, to pick up a Hallmark card at the last minute at the corner drugstore. Her father would never remember her, let alone that today was a holiday.

"There she is." Maven wheeled her father into the community room, and Luna rose to greet them. "Now, Mr. O'Malley, here is your Luna Belle. I know you've been looking forward to seeing her."

"Hi, Daddy."

His hands shook in his lap, and his eyes registered no life. They were flat, distant, and still yellowed from years of alcohol abuse. Perhaps he'd never get rid of the whiskey's effects.

As she moved closer to him, the scent of cotton mixed with his usual stale, sour smell invaded her space.

His gaze lifted to her, and he cocked his head in question.

"It's me, Luna Belle." Every meeting with him began this way. Surely, someday this pattern would cease to roil that hollow pit in her stomach.

Maven gave her a small smile. "Now, you two have a nice

"

visit." She leaned down to talk in her father's ear. "Mr. O'Malley, one of your daughters is getting married today. I'm sure Luna is here to tell you all about it."

"It's Starr who's getting married, Daddy. Catarina." Her sister didn't seem to mind which name Luna shared with him anymore—Starr, her stage name, or Catarina, her birth name. Either way, she'd be Mrs. Nathan Baldwin in a few hours.

Luna pulled up a chair next to him and tentatively put her hand on his forearm. He flinched a little, so she resettled her hands on the card.

"I brought you something." She placed the Valentine in his shaky fingers.

"You sure are pretty. Who...?" His speech hadn't gotten any better, either. He still fumbled his "r's."

"I'm Luna. Starr and Phoenix are your other daughters. Starr is marrying a wonderful man. Nathan. You'd like him." Nathan was more than wonderful, and her sister deserved such a great guy after all she'd been through in the last year.

"You remind me." He raised a bony finger. "A girl I knew. Cara."

Prickles went off in her throat. "That was Mom."

His brow furrowed under a few greasy strands of hair. "Oh, Cara was a sight to behold."

"I know." Luna could recall her long red hair and soft hands, though it was getting harder each year to call up her mother's face in her mind. She tried to think of her often just so she could keep those wispy images from fading anymore.

"I got to meet her later."

"Tell her Happy Valentine's Day." Reminding him her mother died nineteen years ago would be moot.

Luna's phone went off in her purse. Probably Phoenix wondering where she was with Starr's requested bagels and cream cheese. Breakfast of champions, right? But what the bride wanted the bride got on her wedding day.

She'd call Phee from the car because if her sister knew where she was, she'd only get a lecture about lost causes and casting pearls before swine.

Luna stood. "I've got to go, but I'll try to come by in a few days."

"You sure are pretty." Tobacco-stained teeth shone from his mouth, and his arm lifted as if he wanted to touch her. But his hand dropped back in his lap and crinkled the unopened card.

Perhaps Phee was right. What was the point of visiting? He no longer recognized any of them. Luna just hoped to catch him on a good day so she could get her final questions answered—like over the years, had he ever wondered where they were? How they were doing? Was he sorry for all the abuse he heaped on them, especially Phee?

Her eyes drifted to Maven, who kept a watchful eye in the corner. The woman rose, giving her another kind smile, and came forward to collect their father—or what was left of him.

Outside, she cracked open her umbrella to fend off the drizzle. February rain was the saddest rain—gray, cold, with nothing pretty to water, instead spraying oil-slicked streets and umbrellas that had seen too much use already.

At least bad weather on a wedding day meant good luck for the couple—and Lord knew Starr and Nathan deserved every happiness.

Her tennies squeaked against the wet pavement as she hurried back to where she'd parked her car. A black limousine idled across the street. Her heart hitched. Today was Valentine's Day and a Saturday. A thousand limos could be on Baltimore's streets today as romantic paramours tried to impress their dates. It didn't have to be *his*.

She quickly retrieved her keys, but they slipped from her grasp to land in a jangle on the wet pavement in the middle of the street. She crouched down and her umbrella tipped up, sending a long cascade of water onto her back.

The window of the limo lowered in a whine. She made the mistake of looking up. As it always did when she saw him, air died in her lungs. The man with piercing blue eyes and hair as black as night—and hands that when they cradled hers made her heart turn inside out—nodded in her direction.

She'd told him to stop showing up, confusing her, making her soft in the knees. She'd *begged* him.

Scooping up her keys, she rose and looked both ways—to see if anyone might be watching her. Then, hitching her purse strap higher on her shoulder, she strode across the street. She stopped a foot away from where he sat. "Visiting a loved one?"

"Yes."

She dropped her arms. "Oh, I'm sorry."

"I came to see you."

A warmth threatened to rise in her, but she tamped it down with a big mental foot. "You shouldn't have."

"Just five minutes." His door cracked open and stilled her heart—and every other part of her. If he got out, he would bring all his heat—and those mesmerizing blue eyes—closer. He couldn't do that to her, not today.

But he didn't get out. He let the door swing out and hover in the air, ajar. The arrogant bastard slid to the far side of the long seat, so sure she'd enter.

"No." She'd made a deal with herself. As of Starr's wedding day, she'd quit her foolish thoughts—and actions— around Carragh MacKenna. She wouldn't get into his ridiculous limo and bask in the prettiest eyes she'd ever seen on a man, listen to him make small talk, have him ask her about her day, hold her hand. Like they weren't on opposite sides of a growing feud.

Carragh held out his hand, palm up. "Please. Just for a minute." His eyes glittered in the darkened space.

She should walk away. Take a stand for herself. Both of her sisters had found real love in the last year. Luna wanted that kind of love—the kind that protected your heart, not the kind that had you sneak around with a man who was inheriting a mob family legacy.

But the idling of the limo, tires on wet pavement on the street behind her, even the gray exhaust floating in the air behind the car were too loud in her ears. It made it hard to think.

Time to stop this torture. She closed her umbrella and got in with him.

Smooth black leather slid under her fingers. Its rich scent mixed with his Egoiste By Chanel cologne made her head swim just as it had the last three times she'd unwisely slipped into this same car—an outlandish display of wealth and privilege in this day and age.

The door clicked shut and all the sound outside died.

His beard was rough, and fatigue shone in his eyes. It tugged at something in her heart, which was absurd. This man was heir apparent to the mob family that repeatedly threatened and nearly killed everyone she loved—her sisters, their boss, Declan, and her soon-to-be brother-in-law, Nathan.

She settled her purse on her lap. "Pull an all-nighter?"

"Worried about me?" He ran a fingertip over his bottom lip. It was casual, like he hadn't a care in the world. Probably pure bravado on his part.

"Not in the least. You can take care of yourself."

His eyes glanced up at the memory care facility where her father resided. "Everything okay?"

"No. There isn't anything someone can do about Alzheimer's."

The flash of police red and blue lights, barely visible in the tinted glass, sparkled outside.

"You're about to get a ticket." He was parked illegally, of course. Then again, he didn't seem to be the kind of guy who followed the rules ordinary mortals had to.

He laughed. "It'd be worth it. To be sitting here with you."

"Trying to flatter me?" He always did this to her. He tried to charm her with pretty little sayings.

She'd heard every line under the blessed sun. Men who came to watch her dance would wait for her by Shakedown's exit, their eyes filled with hope that somehow, she'd return their interest.

Carragh smiled at her. "Petra."

The driver, who'd barely moved when she got in, turned his face in profile. Petra was an older, distinguished gentleman who looked like a grandfather—or the type she'd always wanted—and not someone who was witness to all Carragh did with his women in the back seat.

Petra lowered his car window, stuck his arm out, and gestured for the cop to move along with two fingers.

The lights died, and the cop drove by.

She glared at Carragh. "I'm not impressed."

"Wasn't trying to impress you."

"What are you trying to do?" Destroy her sanity?

"Can I drop you at your sister's wedding?"

She slowly shook her head. "You shouldn't know about that, Carragh." Or care.

"Why wouldn't I? It's a big day."

"It is." Today didn't get any bigger, and she wouldn't let him pull any more information out of her as he'd done so easily before.

"Please, send my best wishes to your sister and Nathan.

For their wedding day." He reached down to the floorboard and lifted a small box wrapped in white glossy paper and a white ribbed ribbon. The wrapping was classier than she'd expected from a man who'd likely sent people to the bottom of the Patapsco river a time or two… or a hundred.

She didn't take the offering. "They have enough blenders."

"Good. Then this will be something better." He placed it in her lap, and the movement pulled his shirt collar away, bared the red spike of a tattoo on his neck. She'd often wondered what the full image depicted.

"Thank you, but…"

His hand descended on hers. His thumb caressed her skin, slowly, lightly. A hundred messages could be delivered in such a small movement. Care. Interest. Lust. Ownership.

She didn't have time to decipher them.

Can't. Shouldn't. Won't. They were good words to utter at that moment. Instead, she sat there—barely remembering why she got into the limo to begin with.

Oh, right. To end things.

He leaned toward her, unfairly bringing his scent closer—along with his blue eyes that seemed to read every secret she harbored. He lingered inches from her for a long minute.

"A kiss for the bride? You can deliver it for me."

"No." There wouldn't be a time when he could ever kiss her. If he did… well, she couldn't think about that possibility.

"You want me to."

She did—desperately. Without ever having touched his full lips, she already knew what he could do with them.

First, if given permission, he wouldn't hesitate. He'd feast on her mouth, a full takeover, and she'd go willingly once he breached that intimacy.

"This…" she waved her hand between herself and him "… attraction has to stop. We can't. I won't put my sisters in any more danger."

"You and your sisters are in no danger from me."

"And the rest of your family?"

"Will listen to what I say."

"Is that what Ruark did?" The man had held a gun to Starr's head. Beat up Nathan. Went after Declan and Phoenix together. Repeatedly harassed them all.

"He's not getting out for a while."

"But someday."

His brow furrowed and his lack of an answer said it all. There would always be a someday when it came to the MacKenna family and hers. While Carragh would never hurt her—or her sisters—his family would have no trouble cutting out her heart and opening a bottle of Chianti to sip while dining on it.

She'd brought enough misery to Starr and Phee. She wouldn't add more.

"I can't see you..." She grasped the door handle but couldn't seem to turn it. "You can have any woman you want."

She's witnessed them. Even in the Shakedown parking lot, where she worked, glossy-haired, model-thin women entered his limo to later exit with clothes askew, lipstick vanished.

How had they lost it? From his lips or from something else—things she couldn't even think about because her yearning only grew from such imaginings. Unlike him, she couldn't afford the luxury of giving into a mere appetite.

"They aren't you." His hand moved up to her forearm. He gave it a light squeeze, and his eyes searched her face.

"Maybe not, but you're still with them."

He sidled closer, and she raised a hand to stop his advance. "Stop following me. I'm not going to break up my family. Please... stop."

"I can't do that." His hand still had possession of her arm.

She yanked herself free and cracked open the door. "This is the last time you'll see me, Carragh."

His face hardened a bit because, of course, no one ever said "no" to him, right? Certainly not his other women who wore lipstick, dying to have it sucked off. "We'll see about that."

2

———

"Where have you been?" Phoenix grabbed the Martha's Bagels bag from Luna's hand. "Starr's freaking out."

"Traffic. Where is she?"

Phoenix peered into the bag. "Sally Mae is putting finishing touches on her makeup, though it's been touched for, like, three hours. At least she waited until her wedding day to go all Bridezilla."

Cherry waved the steamer. "Luna, love, come help me with this. Hold out the train, I still see a wrinkle. And then we're getting you dressed." She pointed the steamer wand her way.

"The wedding is in three hours. Plenty of time."

"Oh, love, but I don't want you to be *stressed*."

If anyone was stressed, it was Cherry. She tsked and tutted over the nearly invisible wrinkle.

While Phoenix delivered the promised carbs, Luna straightened out the wedding dress' six-foot train. Crystals and a dusting of tiny seed pearls formed a large heart in the center of the piece that would float above a voluminous cloud of snow-white organza and tulle that waterfalled from a fitted, bejeweled corset with a basque waist.

"I still can't get over she didn't go for a mermaid silhouette." Starr had the body for such a form-fitting dress. Even as identical triplets, they varied a little. Starr had always been curvier, Phee a little thinner, and Luna was something in between.

"This dress couldn't be big enough for our Miss Starr." A little tear formed in the corner of Cherry's eye.

"Don't you dare start."

"I can't believe it. One of my babies getting married." Technically, she and her sisters were not Cherry's daughters, but the drag queen had adopted them long ago—thank God. Growing up motherless by age nine was bad. Growing up without a mother only to be placed in foster homes at age eleven thanks to their alcoholic father?

Jesus, why was she thinking about any of that at all?

Cherry fluffed one of the tulle swags on the skirt. "Let's just hope she doesn't take out anyone sitting too close to the aisle."

A laugh burst from Luna's throat, followed by a little choked, happy emotion. Starr had not only found the love of her life but would get to start a family and have a little house someday, and everything would be perfect, perfect, perfect.

"Oh, baby girl." Cherry smooshed Luna to her bosom. After a long hug, she sniffed and then pulled Luna back. "Are you alright? How are you holding up? You look pale."

"I'm fine."

"You saw him today, didn't you?"

Her heart did a little jig. "Who?"

"You may be able to play that innocent little Luna with others, but Momma Cherry sees all." Her face softened. "Carragh MacKenna. There, I said his name—and your eyes did what they always do when that name is uttered out loud."

Luna shook her head. Her eyes hadn't done anything.

"We are standing in a church." She snapped her fingers and wiggled them. "Confess."

Technically, they stood in the fellowship hall, but once Cherry wanted something, that want was eventually fulfilled. "If Carragh keeps showing up, it has nothing to do with me."

Only it did—and she knew it.

"Ah, so you admit you saw him, probably in that throw-back-to-the-90s stretch limo. Such a cliché, on top of the fact he always has some chick in there, getting his rocks lubricated—"

"He's not like that."

Cherry pursed her lips and eyed her. "And how would you know, Miss Luna Belle O'Malley?"

How did she know? She just did.

Despite her desire to stay away from him, Carragh wasn't the monster everyone said. He wasn't like the other MacKenna family members.

His father, Tomas, was the head of a mafia rattlesnake—boastful and prideful. Carragh's one surviving, younger brother, Ruark, was the rattling tail, all bluster and hardness. But Carragh, the eldest son—and the one likely to inherit the legacy—was thoughtful. Also, despite his arrogance, he seemed kind, especially at the most unexpected times.

However, he was still a MacKenna.

Cherry grasped her chin, a motherly gesture. "That car hasn't been idling around the corner of Shakedown every night for just anyone. Oh, yes, I know when you sneak out looking for him."

That was the problem. She didn't look for him. She didn't even need to see his car to know when he was there. She could *feel* him, like ice on the back of her neck but a contrasting heat crawling up her thighs. She'd turn and there he'd be, like last week on Baker Street when she was returning some shoes to that little vintage shop for her sister Phee.

Or the other day when she picked up today's bridesmaids' dresses from the tailor.

Or sometimes he showed up at Shakedown where she danced. His eyes, like two sapphires, would cut through the dark that hid most of the audience. Sometimes he'd grow closer, take a seat by the stage—before Max ushered him to the door. He'd had orders to stay away, repeatedly. He didn't —and showed no remorse for showing up as he was led to the exit.

"Just make sure you don't let Declan or your sisters know about your little tête-a-têtes with that man."

"Of course not." No one could ever know she'd let him within five feet of her. Plus, she'd ended their little flirtation today. "I have to get dressed."

Both of her sisters were happy, and if she had anything to do with it, they'd stay that way. It was her turn to ensure it.

Luna unzipped the garment bag holding her bridesmaid dress. "I just love the colors Starr chose." She ran her hand over the marine blue silk.

"Well, it certainly solves the 'something blue' thing." Cherry waved her hand.

Both she and Phee would walk up the aisle in two-tone cocktail dresses reflecting the bridal colors—a lighter turquoise and a darker marine blue. The bodices were fitted with a large V cut down to their navels, the edges and trim lined with silver sparkles. Luna especially loved the skirt's silk Fortuny pleats that moved like waves when they walked.

Cherry, however? Starr had given her free rein on the design of her matron-of-honor dress, which was all Cherry had to hear to reserve every turquoise and blue Swarovski crystal in all of Baltimore for her custom-made, form-fitting gown. She was spectacular in the dress. "A fountain of Caribbean waters," Starr had called it.

A huge gasp came from Cherry, who then slapped both hands to her sternum.

Luna turned to find Starr swishing the hem of her dress in front a three-paneled mirror.

It didn't matter what any of them wore. All eyes would be on Starr in her wedding gown. Light reflected in waves over the chiffon, and later, when she walked down the aisle, the cathedral train would float above the voluminous skirt, the sparkles catching the lights like stars.

But it was her hair, like fire and copper, flowing down her back and bare shoulders with thin strands of crystals intertwined in her curls, that made her otherworldly like a mermaid come to life.

Starr's eyes caught hers in the mirror. "What do you think?"

Luna's throat squeezed and she nodded. Starr didn't need the mermaid silhouette after all. "You're a princess."

"Don't you dare cry," she choked. "You'll smear your make-up."

Phee, who had sidled up next to Luna, slipped her fingers into her hand. "You're perfect."

In a rustle of tulle, Starr flounced over to them and grasped both of her sisters' wrists. "Sisters forever, friends always."

"Amen," Phoenix said.

Luna just nodded, her throat oddly closing more by the second.

"Oh, baby girl…" Cherry just tsked. "Nathan is one lucky stud."

Starr cocked a hip. "Don't I know it." She then gazed over at Phoenix. "Next time it will be you."

Phee just rolled her eyes. "Let's not get ahead of

ourselves." As if the six years it took for her to admit her love for Declan was rushing things?

"And you too, L." Starr bumped her with her shoulder. "We're all going to live on the same street someday. I just know it."

Yes, they would. Because she'd find a man who wasn't about to become the head of a crime family. Even if Carragh's face never fully left her mind or the warmth of his fingers around hers still seemed alive in her skin even now when holding her sisters' hands.

3

____

"So, if you lay down a little stronger incentive…"

Carragh silenced the man with his hand. Sean let a sigh rumble in this throat. He'd been after Carragh to get engaged in the pending deal with his family and the Monroe family for the last hour. "It can wait."

Sean glanced out the window and gave a tight nod. "Want me to get out with you?"

A heaviness filled Carragh's chest. "No."

From his window, Carragh stared across the cemetery's expanse of brown winter grass. Dirty white concrete lumps and spires pointed upward. He didn't really see any of them except one, a tall, granite angel whose robes, expertly carved, draped down the pedestal on which she stood.

Such utter crap since his mother had never been treated like an angel—rather more like a pawn by two warring families who sought to create an alliance only to have the partnership tumble like children's building blocks. His father was a child, always wanting more, throwing his toys—even his late wife—away if he might lose.

He had hoped his father would evolve. Their new partners, like the Monroes, wouldn't take kindly to his legendary temper tantrums.

Sean cleared his throat.

"Something else?" He glanced at his cousin and watchdog over Tomas MacKenna's only remaining son. Technically, the "only" part wasn't true, but Ruark landed his ass in a mental institution to avoid jail. It marred his standing with their father. Namely, removed him from the family crest.

"I'm a little worried about you." Sean raised his hand. "There, I said it."

"Nothing to concern yourself with."

"But the dancer…"

Every muscle, tendon, and joint in his body seized. "What dancer?"

Sean rolled his head to one side in a come-on gesture. "The redhead we've been not so conveniently driving by for weeks. It was why you were late picking me up, wasn't it? That Starr chick got married today. You went by?"

He wasn't about to share squat with Sean. He'd only get a lecture, which would be rich given he'd had to yank the guy out of Shakedown, where the girls danced, more than once.

"That what you've been reporting in to my father?" Tomas MacKenna often knew where his son was. Frankly, he knew quite too much these days.

"No, man, I wouldn't—"

"No?"

The man's nostrils flared. "No."

Carragh stared at the man for one long minute. His cousin could lie with the best of them—but not as well as Carragh. He'd been doing it his whole life.

Truth told, he probably shouldn't keep seeking out Luna Belle, but she reeled him in with the most lethal bait. Every fiber of her body said she wanted him, but her pretty lips kept saying "no."

No one said "no" to him, and certainly no one of the female variety.

Then there was her mouth. Sure, her eyes, her body, would make most men drop to their knees. But the way she twisted those pink lips when he stared at her. His gut twisted with the knowledge she wanted him to kiss her—hard. But her strength of will proved far greater than her desire, another of her qualities he fucking loved. The woman had standards.

He had to stop thinking of her or he'd grow hard. Given he was in the car with only men, it would prove… awkward. "I'm getting some air. Stay here."

Before Carragh could even reach for the door handle, his driver cracked his door and moved to get out to start the drill: open Carragh's door, hold an umbrella over him. Carragh would grasp the umbrella handle to signal he didn't need an escort. As usual, Petra would voice stuttered protests, but Carragh would win his independence. It was an irrational daily ritual he'd been doing every Sunday since his mother died—at least when he was in town.

If their enemies wanted him dead, they could have taken their shot at him—a man standing alone over a mother's grave—long ago.

Carragh lifted himself out of the back before Petra could even open the umbrella. He grasped it from the man's hand. "I've got it."

"But sir—"

"Petra."

The man nodded once and clasped his hands before him. He'd watch him stride up the walkway, make a right thirteen grave makers in, and walk the forty-three steps to the granite angel.

Carragh stood on the soggy grass, his shoes sinking so far into the soil his socks grew wet. He and Sean would be striding into his father's office later. With any luck, he'd leave a little of the mud on the man's precious Oriental, a reminder of where Tomas damned well already knew he'd be today—and where he, the man who was once married to her, couldn't bother to show up.

The telltale click of keys jangled behind him. Sean would never learn, would he? Sounds like that could get a man killed if he was trying to stay hidden.

The sky continued to spit water down on them, the tiny tings of heavy drops striking their umbrellas.

Sean finally spoke. "My mother's coming by later. Asked her to wait a bit."

"Thanks." The guy would know Carragh wanted to be the first to visit his mother's grave before the wailing would start from Sean's mother, his aunt.

Twenty years ago today, Catherine Elizabeth MacKenna was laid in this grave. Her maiden name, Flynn, wasn't part of her marker. Another of his father's decrees. Once a MacKenna only a MacKenna.

Carragh began his ritual. First, take in each letter of her name. Then recall her warm smile, a touch of her hand. The memories were growing hazier every year. He scrubbed his face. Shit, did it have to rain today?

"It's Petra."

The two words made Carragh's head swivel to Sean.

What was the man talking about? "Talk."

"Ever wonder why he suddenly wanted to start driving you all the time? Instead of me? Caught him in your father's office a few weeks ago. Didn't think anything of it until… ya know, your dad getting on you about the dancer." He shielded his face with the umbrella from the limo behind him, though it was far enough away lip-reading was out of the question by a 70-year-old man.

"So what?"

Really, so what if he reported Carragh couldn't seem to shake an obsession with a certain redhead with legs for miles —legs he'd fight ten men to get the chance to have wrapped around him.

"Yeah, but then the cash. Hand to hand delivery."

"Doesn't mean anything," he lied. It meant everything. Cash was handed over for only very good reasons, like vital information that might put someone six feet under. If he was being paid to report in, he'd want more than a name of who Carragh wanted to fuck.

"Maybe not. Maybe so." Sean eyed him, his face taking on an eerie bluish tint from the sky's glom and the navy umbrella.

Carragh ripped his gaze away from the man back to the grave marker.

Petra. It was one betrayal he couldn't fathom. The man had been with the family for a generation, been Carragh's first driver, taking him to school starting when he was ten years old, and things finally had turned ugly. Then he'd stepped up, offered to drive him during the week, not just the weekends, something about needing to feel useful again.

Perhaps his father had something on him. A late-night to Maxim's for a prostitute? Medical bills for his wife, a sweet, round woman who snuck Carragh cookies after school when his father declared the house off-limits due to some particularly hostile meeting? Did it really matter?

If Petra was feeding his father scraps about his sex life, big fucking deal. If his father got wind of other meetings, however…

Sean squared himself to the grave. "I'll keep an eye on him."

"Not a hair." Until he had hard evidence, the man wouldn't be touched.

In his periphery, Sean nodded once.

"That goes for everyone at Shakedown, too. We're staying away." Though he couldn't seem to do that himself. Just to check to make sure his father wasn't seeking to remove another family thorn in his side—namely, long-lost cousin Declan Phillips, Shakedown's owner. He'd ordered Carragh to send some messages, which he refused to do. It was petty bullshit, and he had better things to do.

"Understood there was a truce of sorts."

"Of sorts." His father hadn't yet managed to keep one intact, however.

Carragh glanced at his watch and turned away. He and Sean had a "late lunch" with dear old Dad. In reality, it was likely a strategy session to lay out the response to the latest pressures from some external forces the man didn't like. He was so fucking sick of getting orders from his father.

Sean didn't budge, so he paused his exit. "Something else?"

"I'll follow you."

Carragh arched an eyebrow, and out of habit used his umbrella as a shield between him and the car.

"When you make your move," he continued.

The rain on nylon pinged in his ears. He stared up at the gray sky, contemplating the best reaction he could make.

This wasn't a conversation he wanted to have with Sean right now. The man had been his friend and confidante his whole life, but loyalty to the MacKennas meant loyalty to only one man—Tomas, his father. At least to date.

"Where'd you hear I'm moving?"

Sean shrugged. "Lucky guess."

Perhaps. "You overhear something?"

"No."

Sean's words unsettled him. Only two people knew of his desires—to finally take his rightful place on the MacKenna throne, not to the left of it. They were Petra—because he overheard things—and Declan Phillips, who he'd unwisely revealed his plans to some time ago. He doubted Declan had truly understood Carragh's words that day when the words slipped free from him.

If Sean guessed his plans, people around them also had—and were talking. His father's retirement was long overdue, but it'd be on Carragh's time. Things were just… complicated.

Then there was the matter of a certain burlesque dancer. He wasn't yet sure if he wanted to keep her away from him or get her under him. But he knew this: once he got a taste of her, he'd shoot his own father to protect her if needed. But then, it wouldn't be the first time he'd shot one of his own.

So, yeah, timing was critical.

"We'll be late." Carragh turned away.

4

———

"We're maaaaried." Starr swayed a little on the stage, her dress swaying in time with her.

Nathan caught her from falling off her heels. "We are, baby." He sported the largest grin Luna had ever seen on the man. In fact, she'd not seen either of them so… light. Much of Starr's exuberance was probably from the three glasses of champagne, but then she'd always been the most vocal of the three of them.

"To us!" Starr raised her glass high and the sixty guests on Shakedown's main floor raised flutes, tumblers, and in Luna's case, a glass of sparkling water spiked with lemon and lime.

Cherry Noir entered stage left because no stage was complete without her, according to the performer herself. "May the happy couple reign and rule over their days so long as time exists."

"So be it," Luna said under her breath and took a sip.

Pop. Another champagne bottle opened, and a loud cheer went up as Jackie, who stood on a chair, poured the bubbly into the top glass of the champagne fountain, built by Declan himself. The crystal tinged and chimed as the champagne overflowed from glass to glass.

Cherry moved to Cortelana, who stood regal in a bejeweled tuxedo. Enough sparkles and feathers to put on a show shone under the dimmed spotlights hanging from the girders. Declan had put gold and pink filters on all the lights so it bathed everyone in a glow that mirrored the happy energy filling the room.

Huge flowers hung from the ceiling, giving it an air of part circus, part elegant British tea, and the tables were draped in blue and gold bunting, giving it a regal but festive air. Boisterous jazz music filled the room, and no one could seem to stand still.

Little feathers in Sally Mae's vintage pillbox fluttered as Aspen swung her in time with the music. Rachel bounced little Nicolas on her hip as he giggled and waved his chubby arms in the air.

Maybe she would let Luna hold baby Nicolas again. She'd held him all through dinner—a big, squishy bundle in a little man suit. Luna reluctantly handed him back to his mother when he started to fuss and Rachel asked for him back. She could have held the baby all day if Rachel had wanted— crying or not.

Across the room, Phee's assistant, Naomi, a former stripper her sister rescued from Maxim's last year, talked with Nathan's young daughter, Madeline. The young girl, dressed in head-to-toe pink, hung on every word from Naomi, who was probably selling her on dance classes at Phee's school. Not a bad idea given Madeline visited her father and Starr often.

Luna's eyes searched the room for Phoenix. Her heartbeat danced a little at seeing her banded tightly to Declan in a morning suit, complete with matching cane. Of course, he was never far from her sister, and that fact quieted things in her.

Phee's eyes still cast doubt toward him now and again as if she couldn't realize a true gentleman—and Declan was one of the best—could possibly have chosen her to give his heart to.

Her sisters deserved all the happiness the world had to offer—even if it meant they were embarking on lives without her. At least they danced together now and again, though it was far less than even last year.

Phoenix was busy with her own dance school next door. Starr couldn't stop talking about starting a family. As for Luna? She was happy where she was—mostly. At least when she wasn't having Carragh MacKenna's presence cutting into her peace. Damn him for showing up today of all days.

A tumbler with brown liquid—attached to a huge hand and even larger forearm—swirled in her vision. The ice clinked as Max shook it.

Luna twisted to face him. "Thanks. But you know I don't drink."

"You look like today would be a good time to start."

Had her face registered that last thought about Carragh? "What the hell." She took it and sniffed.

He laughed. "It's rum and Diet Coke. Thought you might like it."

She took a sip. "Mmm, sweet."

"Like you."

Uh-oh. "Thanks, Max. I'm going to go check on Starr. It's almost time." Time for Starr and Nathan to head on their honeymoon and time for her to make an exit before Max, clearly under the influence, made an unwise move. For years she thought he was just being nice, not really interested in her.

He had such a sweet heart under all those tattoos and

brawn. But he'd be happy with her off-stage and tucked away in some small row house where they'd live a quiet life, unlike another man with piercing blue eyes.

She quickly sidled up to Phee. "Think putting her on a boat is a good idea?" She lifted her chin toward Starr, who was being carried off stage by Nathan, white fabric nearly engulfing his legs. Only Starr would want to honeymoon on a sailboat.

Phee laughed. "Nathan will put a life preserver on every limb, though given that dress? It could drown a Navy SEAL."

"Let's go get her changed before we test that theory."

Declan gave her a peck on the cheek. "Go. I'll attend to the masses."

Her sister flushed from head to toe. He was the only man in the world who could elicit such a reaction from Phee.

They managed to get Starr unhooked from Nathan's arms and to the dressing room. They walked in on Sally holding a white knit dress with a faux fur collar. Cherry had a steamer wand in her hand. She must have found a winkle threatening to rise.

"What?" Cherry demanded. "She has to look perfect for her exit."

"Yes, I do." Starr swept her arms and then caught the flash of her diamond wedding ring in her periphery. She brought her hand back down, wistfully contemplated the ring. "Wow. I'm really Midnight Starr Baldwin now."

"She's just now getting this?" Phee asked Luna.

She eased Starr down to the stool, which disappeared under the billow of crystal-encrusted white tulle. "You are Catarina Baldwin. And Midnight Starr."

"I'm all of it now." She peered up at them with dreamy eyes, then slapped her lap in a muffled rustle. "Okay, get me out of this thing and put me in something sexier. I want him trying to rip my clothes off the second he sees me."

"Like that's any different from any other day?" Phee laughed.

"But no more storeroom shenanigans," Luna added. Starr and Nathan had a penchant for disappearing during his breaks and were once caught *in flagrante delicto* by Trick, the club's manager.

With some difficulty, they managed to get her wedding dress unhooked and slithered off Starr. Getting her into the knit dress was far easier.

They returned to the front of the club where Nathan grasped Starr's hand immediately, a huge grin lighting up his face. As soon as they stepped outside, they were pelted with rose petals and bird seed from the guests who'd gathered in the misty afternoon. It didn't stop Starr from hugging everyone goodbye at least twice, her low heels crunching on the layer of seeds littering the walkway. Eventually, Nathan lifted her off her feet into his arms and headed toward the car.

"Wait!" Starr waved her bouquet of white roses, delphinium, and eucalyptus over his shoulder. "I have to throw it." She then threw it with a force worthy of the Orioles lead pitcher—right at Phee, who gasped when the bouquet landed in her arms.

Rose petals and the smaller delphinium petals peppered the sidewalk next as Phee just stared at it like she couldn't understand what it was. Declan grinned widely but wisely didn't drop onto one knee to propose right then and there.

Luna knew someday Phee would capitulate to marriage, and Declan was anything but impatient.

As Starr and Nathan's car drove away, the *Just Married* sign that Madeline had decorated, complete with blue sparkles, flapped in the wind, and a few of the guests jogged behind, clapping and whooping.

Phee looped her arm into Luna's, the bouquet dropped by

her side. "Wow. It really happened." She glanced at Luna. Her eyes were rimmed in red.

"It did."

"It's one week," Cherry waved her champagne glass. "And y'all will be at each other's houses every other night like you always are."

"You're just saying all that so you won't cry." Phee bumped her with the flowers.

Cherry gently took the bouquet, probably to save it from losing any more blooms. She brought the flowers to her nose. "It took me two hours for this face, I'm not about to ruin it now."

Still, Luna had seen plenty of tears welling in Cherry's eyes at the church.

"I'll mist the bouquet so it doesn't wilt anymore. And two words for you..." Cherry waggled her finger in the air. "... waterproof lashes. I learned my lessons with you three years ago."

The three of them had been through a lot—and Cherry had always been by their side. She hadn't had it easy, either. Being turned out by your family for her gender fluidity? They had no idea who they were missing. Cherry was one of the most beautiful humans to grace this planet.

Declan sidled up to Phee. "Ready to go?"

"Yes," Luna said. "You two go. I'll stay and help clean up."

"No need. That's what the catering staff is for. We're closed tomorrow, so you should probably go out with Max and the rest of the dancers. I hear there's an after-party brewing." Declan winked at her.

"I may be a little partied out."

Phee turned to her. "You sure you're going to be okay? Declan and I don't have to go to the cabin, you know."

No." She hugged her sister. "Go. Have a great rest of the weekend. I'm fine."

She nodded once and turned back to go retrieve her things. From the shelter of the awning, Luna looked out at the mist still falling and their friends laughing and smiling as they strode to their cars.

Declan stood with her. He rocked onto his cane. "See Carragh today?"

"Cherry told you." Because of course, she had. Overprotective as ever.

"She didn't need to. I've seen him hovering around. You see him today?"

She shrugged. She *so* did not want to get into this conversation today. "Told him to stay away."

"Good. He's dangerous."

"Don't worry about me, Declan. He'd never hurt me." She didn't know how she knew that, but she was certain of her safety around him. He was no threat to her—except her virtue, sanity, and body.

"You can't ask me to stop worrying." He inclined his head to the club. "Come on. We'll give you a lift home."

"I've got my car."

His brow furrowed.

She ran her hand down his arm. "I'm fine. Just going to stand here and get some air. Go inside."

"I'll send Max to wait with you."

"No," she said quickly. She didn't need a bodyguard and she certainly didn't need Max getting any wrong ideas. "Just need a minute to think." She winked at him.

He finally got the hint, and as soon as the etched glass door swung closed behind him, an urge to move her limbs overtook her. A stand had been set out, stocked with mismatched umbrellas. Declan thought of everything. She grasped one and clicked it open. A walk would do her good.

To think once Shakedown was the only place worth visiting in this section of town. Since Declan had opened the club, however, this whole stretch of waterfront had become sort of an entertainment district. Henry's Jazz Cafe down the street, Phee's dance studio next door, and a few other entertainment venues that'd opened recently made it feel safer than the old, long stretch of abandoned warehouses from years ago.

Today, the street was quiet as most of the entertainment venues only opened at night. It'd be buzzing with cars and people soon enough.

For now, she'd just enjoy the relative stillness, and before she knew it, she'd walked two blocks.

Henry's Jazz Cafe was dark. Sooty marks still marred the side of the building where a fire had tried to take down the whole place last year. Trash had piled up near the side wall.

Across the street, graffiti—big arcs of red and white paint in strange symbols—marred the warehouse. Funny how she never felt unsafe here despite the low-rent vibe.

Her heel caught in a crack in the sidewalk. "Damn it." She should have changed shoes. Her toes had begun to pinch, too.

Her coat hemline lashed her legs as she took long strides up the familiar street. She rubbed her arms together. Her thin trench coat was no match for the February weather. Turning around, however, wasn't an option. Her head was too... full.

Surely, the air would clear her mind, work out some of the odd melancholy that had risen up in her chest. A chapter of her and her sisters' lives were closing and she was helpless to stop it. That fact made her ordinary. It happened to everyone, right? Still, her stomach would not settle as if she'd boarded some proverbial roller-coaster with no idea when the next turn or hill would send her careening around her seat.

Her thoughts began to drift—a jumble of images more than anything. Her father shrunken in a wheelchair. Starr's radiant face as she proclaimed—rather loudly—"I do" today. Then icy blue eyes that she may never have to look at again. She just wasn't sure she was happy about that last one.

But life changes on a dime, isn't that what everyone said?

Really, she should have been more prepared for an emotional day. Starr getting married was a huge milestone in their lives. She just thought she'd have more control over her reaction.

She rubbed her sternum and the ache that had settled just under it.

"Get a grip," she said aloud. She needed to focus more on the bright side of things. Her sisters were happy. She had a good job that she loved. She had a family. Soon, she ceased to see the gray sky overhead or the wind that picked up a notch.

Perhaps that's why she didn't notice when the car started following her. By the time she did, it was too late.

5

———

Carragh stood in front of his father's desk. His father hadn't looked up from the ledger he studied since Carragh had arrived. Sean plopped himself down on the small leather couch to the side but Carragh had no intention of staying longer than necessary.

"Well?" The man still hadn't glanced up.

Sean leaned forward, elbows to knees. "We discussed it and—"

"Did I ask you?"

Sean gave Carragh a half-smile and sank back in the seat. His cousin, familiar with his uncle's drill, had learned to shrug off Tomas' curt nature long ago.

Tomas tapped a pen against the paper he couldn't seem to rip his gaze from. "You didn't do what I asked."

No question. Just a statement of fact because they both knew Carragh had damned well belayed his over-the-top orders. Sending Declan a scare message—during a wedding, to boot—was a move made by a man having a temper tantrum.

"If you don't, I'll do it myself." His father looked up. One eye twitched. The man was having one of his legendary migraines. Good.

"Feel free."

Tomas' lips inched up and he chuffed. "Sit, Carragh. Say what's on your mind. Then we'll eat."

"Not hungry." Tomas didn't summon him here for a friendly family lunch. His true motivation would eventually reveal itself.

"A shame. Mary cooked pulled beef."

"Where were you today?" The anniversary of his wife's death at least deserved a graveside visit.

"I'd ask the same of you. You didn't just go to your mother's gravesite, did you?"

His father scrutinized him, but he wouldn't find anything on his face. Carragh had schooled out his facial reactions years ago. "You know damned well."

"Yes, your proclivity for certain redheads hasn't waned."

"Where did you hear that?"

The man's chair squeaked a little as he leaned back. "Your choice in women is important."

Ah, so they were playing this game today. "Didn't think you cared who I fucked."

That got a flinch out of him.

The man's lips thinned. "Choosing a mate is the single most critical decision of your life."

"Is that what you thought when you married my mother?"

It was a marriage of convenience. That much Carragh knew. "Your mother was a good wife." His chair thunked upright.

"That why you didn't bother to go see her today?"

He slammed his fist down. "You know nothing."

"Maybe because you don't tell me anything." Carragh never knew exactly what happened that fateful day her life ended.

"As you don't. Like why you would jeopardize our family—"

"Jeopardize? You mean like taking out your own kin, Declan?"

"I have never suggested such a thing." He eyed Carragh's chest. Thought he was wired? He wished he was. But what would that do? Only put him on the outs with the other families. The man had loyalties built—even if they were, at best, tenuous.

His father rounded the desk and stopped just in front of him.

For a long minute, they eyed one another until the sound of Sean's jeans sliding on the leather as he moved forward filled the air. As if he was readying himself to jump between them, perhaps. The only question was who he'd protect. Despite Sean's declaration in the cemetery, Carragh knew better than to trust words.

"If I can't count on you, then..." His father lifted one shoulder in a delicate shrug.

"Then what? I never said you couldn't, but I have my own ways of doing things."

"Yes, your independent streak has been showing itself lately. But if you don't have your family's back, then you're not a man. We take care of our own."

Interesting that he considered harassing Declan, his nephew, care. Then there was the matter of his other son, Ruark, who went rogue and was now *persona non grata* with their father.

"And Ruark?"

The man broke eye contact and sighed. "Even him." His father eventually came around and agreed to foot the guy's medical bills even if he said Ruark would never darken his door again.

Tomas stretched, strode to the door, and opened it. "Come on. Mary's got it ready for us."

In the end, Carragh would sit at his father's table. Eat pulled beef like nothing's happening on the streets, like they were one big happy family.

Family. It'd shrunk over the years.

First, his mother's chair stood absent. Then his youngest brother's, Daniel, who they lost to some stupid fight. Then, Ruark, who'd gone mad with revenge, landed himself in a mental institution. Cousins had drifted away. And Declan? The long-lost cousin hidden from Tomas all those years? Now he was in plain sight and refused to join the family fold.

They played the family game anyway.

As his father poured red wine into goblets, Mary, their long-time housekeeper, fussed around Sean and Carragh, dishing out three times the amount any human should eat in one sitting of roasted potatoes with parsley, pulled beef, green beans with walnuts, and baked yams. Too bad his conversation with his father had everything sit like dust on his tongue.

"Mary," Tomas waved his hand over the spoon she held out with another helping of potatoes. "I'm about to burst."

"Well, just make sure you leave room for my cherry pie. It's almost done. I should go check." She scooted out.

"Take your time."

Mary nodded once. She understood the order—"We'll call you when we need you, but don't enter otherwise." His father didn't make suggestions.

Carragh glanced out the wavy leaded glass windows. Smears of water clouded the view, but what was there to see? A street worthy of a postcard with ordinary upper-class families living their ordinary lives inside the neighboring homes. Carragh often wondered if their neighbors knew what their father did for a living.

The street was far too good for the man he now broke bread with.

His father fiddled with the stem of his wine goblet, the blood-red glow in the glass making his fingers redden from the dimmed overhead lighting. "About the Monroes."

"What about them? Heard they brokered a deal without you. It's business."

"Except that section of cove is ours." He lifted his ever-present cell phone, glanced at the screen, and let it drop back to the table surface. "Once we're in partnership, I need to know you're up to the task to make sure it goes our way. His daughter—"

"I thought you had no interest in waterfront properties." He didn't want to hear any more about Monroe's eldest girl who everyone hoped he'd fall for. Or, rather, at least put in his bed with the marriage certificate hanging over it.

"Let's say my son has changed my mind. You certainly spend a lot of time there."

"I enjoy the entertainment. All work and no play makes for a dull life."

"Is that what Luna Belle O'Malley is to you? Play?"

The sound of her name on his lips stiffened his whole body. "She's one of many." In fact, he'd made damn sure people saw him out with women often. Focusing on any one could make her an easy target. "I'm a little old for the fatherly sex talk, don't you think?"

"You always were a precocious kid. Your mother worried about the babysitters." He laughed.

The fact he uttered "your mother" chilled his spine.

His father took a sip of his wine. "I'm surprised you'd go for someone so beneath you."

If the man believed he could goad him into revealing what he was up to, he was mightily wrong. "I haven't gone for anyone."

"You need to. At your age, I had three sons."

"Yes, and now you're down to two." Bringing up Daniel's death was a low blow but he was done pulling punches.

He pulled out his cell phone, tapped out a message. "Let's make sure I'm not down anymore."

The sound of the front door opened along with footsteps. But they were no ordinary footsteps. The heavy thunk of the men that came and went in this household was mixed with a delicate click of heels.

He turned in his chair and his gaze immediately met bright blue eyes. They darted around the room as if they couldn't quite figure out where she was.

Luna. Terrence had a tight grip on her arm as he led her in. Or rather pulled her.

"Let go of me," she seethed. Her hair hung in long wet rivulets, a blue dress stuck to her breasts under an open trench coat.

Terrence didn't ease his grip one bit. Carragh would kill the man for that rough handling.

He had two options. He could stand, dash to the woman's rescue. Or he could do what would work. She was now officially on Tomas MacKenna's radar screen, and he had put her there. He could get her out.

Carragh casually turned his head to his father. "So, is this my Valentine's Day present? You shouldn't have."

Tomas affixed a smug smile on his face and leaned back in his chair. "Well, you always did have good taste in women. So, I thought I'd give her a go."

This was beyond goading. He was laying down the gauntlet, daring him to pick up a sword and fight him.

His father's death—right here, right now—would feel so fucking good. Brains splattered on the back wall. Blood leaking out of his nose, mouth, and the bullet hole he'd place right in the center of his cold heart.

"How dare you," Luna hissed.

In his periphery, he saw Luna pulling her coat tighter to her. Of course, she was scared—and pissed.

This entire set-up was a show—one that said Tomas could pick up Luna anytime, do what he wanted. To show Carragh he would always be one step behind and in reaction mode.

Well, no longer. Carragh took his time slipping more air into his lungs and schooled his face to the mask he'd perfected over the years. "Checking in with me? Asking permission?"

His father's face hardened with dissatisfaction and then he stood. "Put her over there." He inched his chin toward the extra dining room chairs that flanked a large credenza. She wasn't even going to get a seat at the table. The situation was worse than he knew.

Luna's eyes fired. "No one's *putting* me anywhere." She jerked her arm free. "Now, someone want to tell me why the hell I got pushed into a car and brought here? I thought the MacKennas' kidnapping days were over."

She glared hard at Carragh in particular.

He had to give her credit. She was furious. He knew better. She had to also be terrified under that veneer. Good for her for not showing it.

Sean palmed his wine glass and wisely remained mute. He appeared bored, though his eyes darted around the room as if seeking an escape.

"Carragh, you can sit down now." His father's voice was exceedingly calm given the thoughts running through Carragh's mind.

Carragh hadn't even realized he had slowly risen from his seat. His hands were clenched into fists and no matter what he did he couldn't seem to unclench them. Try as he might, he couldn't be anything but honest around this woman. His body's inability to lie around her was gonna be a real fucking problem.

His father turned to him. "Now, I'm going to explain to you two why you'll never be together. Not if you want to stay alive."

6

Sitting? She didn't think so.

Luna marched to the large bay window overlooking the front yard, a half-acre at least of sprawling grass leading down to the street. "You know if I disappear or show up harmed, the police will only arrive at your doorstep first."

The rain had stopped as quickly as it came up that morning. If she tried to run, though, she'd still slip and fall in her heels.

She'd throw them off and make a run for it.

That wouldn't work, either. She couldn't outrun the stocky man with the strong Boston accent, a detail she'd learned long ago to mark when it came to strange men just in case she had to report it later.

"Miss O'Malley, please have a seat." Tomas MacKenna's voice swept over her like greasy hands.

"I'll stand." Though her feet were killing her, she wasn't taking orders from him.

She shuddered a little, still cold. She hadn't dressed properly for her impromptu walk. But then she didn't expect she was going far from Shakedown until a car slowed by her, the passenger door opening, and an order to get inside.

She'd spun on her heel to head back when the screech of brakes sounded, followed by a car door slam.

She'd tried to run but nearly fell off her heels when the man caught her. He told her to shut up, that Carragh wanted to see her.

"Have it your way," Tomas said.

She glanced over at him. "Well, then I would like for you to call me a taxicab."

The man had the gall to chuckle.

Carragh hadn't said another word.

"Okay. Carragh can drive me. Your guy said he wanted to see me." She must have been channeling her sister Phoenix somehow. She was never this brave.

As a child, Phoenix always took the brunt of their father's abuse. And Starr had certainly taken the brunt of the MacKenna's abuse last year. Well, no more. She wasn't going to be abused and she wasn't going to be intimidated.

"Father, you done with the drama yet?" Carragh's words were stopped when Tomas lifted his hand to silence him.

"Not until you listen to me. And then Sean will drive Miss O'Malley anywhere she wants to go." Tomas swaggered over to her.

She continued to stare out over the grounds, not really seeing anything. For long minutes the two of them stood there staring out over his front yard. She worked hard to still her muscles. She would not tremble in front of this man.

"You have a nice place. It doesn't suit you."

In her periphery, she caught Tomas staring at her profile. "My wife chose this house."

"Where is she? I'd like to meet her." Something about seeing another woman might make her feel better. As if the presence of a female might make this man behave better? Who was she kidding?

"My wife passed some time ago."

Ah, that's right. She knew that, but no one could expect her brain to be working at full throttle. "I'm sorry. When did she die?"

"Carragh was fourteen."

She turned to face his profile. "How?"

"Bullet."

She swallowed thickly. She was stupid to ask him.

"And that is why, Miss O'Malley…" his steely eyes moved to his son. "…you two will never see each other again."

His words made no sense but whatever. "Fine by me." Luna began to move for the door, but she was completely stopped in her tracks at Carragh's next words.

"It's not fine."

Tomas' brows arched. "And what do you think your future wife will think of your late-night excursions?"

Luna stared at Carragh, anger clawing up her spine. Engaged, of course. She pitied the woman who spent her days seeking this man's attention. An annoying sliver of envy arose, too. Who was this mysterious fiancée who spent her nights with him? Who had his ice-blue eyes look down on her as he pressed her into the mattress? She wondered if any of them had been one of the women she'd seen sitting in his limo.

She ripped her eyes from him. Her fear was making her crazy. It was impossible she could care about anything in this man's life.

She was in danger—real danger, like Starr had been under the hands of Ruark MacKenna. And then Declan and Phoenix months later. She'd always believed Carragh was better, though, making peace, checking on her and Shake-down to see if they were okay.

Now, she knew the truth. He saw her like so many had in her past—like a commodity to be toyed with. A nothing. One of his limo bimbos.

It'd all been a setup—lure them into thinking everything was going to be okay and then you're whisked off the street and deposited in front of the head of the snake.

The snake then spoke. "You see, Miss O'Malley, my son is in line to inherit our family business. That means his choice of who he spends time with reflects on everyone in the family. And my son is already spoken for. His mother arranged it."

That raised an angry chuckle from Carragh's throat. "She did no such thing. Nicole and I are not engaged, Father. You know this."

"Her family would disagree. They are a little, say, agitated that you've waited this long."

"You do realize we're in the 21st century?"

"Where one's word still counts for something."

Carragh joined her by her side, took her arm, and steered her toward the door. "Come on. I'll get you home."

His hand wrapped around her bicep, so strong and so warm; heat seeped right through her thin coat and dress to her skin.

"No. I can—"

He growled low in her ear. "You will do this."

7

———

"I apologize. This won't happen again." Carragh's long black coat flapped in the wind like a villain as he held open the door to a dark blue sedan.

"I'd rather walk." She whirled away, but her foot, soaked from walking in the misty rain, slid in her shoe and she stumbled. His arms reached out and grasped her. Her back slammed into his chest, and his hands tightened around her biceps. Jesus, he was strong.

He murmured in her ear. "Get in the car. We are being watched."

She jerked herself free, and she resumed her walk—away from him, away from the car.

A low huff sounded behind her, followed by the slam of a car door. She had to move slowly, and she reminded herself to throw these shoes out later. They were ruined—as if it mattered.

For long minutes, they tread slowly along the wet sidewalk. The clouds above had begun to clear a bit, but it was still cold. She hugged her arms to herself. There had to be a main road nearby where she could get a cab. Or better still, why hadn't she just called a car service from her phone by now? Oh, maybe because it was *back at Shakedown.* She really wasn't thinking today.

Carragh shrugged out of his coat and held it up to her. "Don't be a fool. Just take it."

Fine, if he wanted to freeze while he played gentleman, so be it. "I am not a fool." She turned her back on him and he settled it over her shoulders, warm, male scent and that delicious cologne enveloping her along with his body heat. The coat's hem nearly touched the ground on her, and she wasn't short.

"I know you're not." A whisper of his hand across his chin sounded in her ear, made her tingle.

She faced him. "Do you?"

A car engine rumbled in the air, and the blue sedan she was *not* getting into began to inch alongside them. She recognized the man sitting in the driver's seat as the guy sitting silently at the table during her confrontation with Tomas.

Jesus, she'd said those things to Tomas MacKenna. This family made her voice and do all kinds of things she didn't think possible.

"It's just Sean."

Like that was supposed to make her feel better? "I recognize him from Shakedown." He and his friend got so drunk once, they'd reached for Phoenix when she was on stage.

She resumed her walk, the movement making her feel better. She hugged the back of her arms more tightly to her under Carragh's coat and glanced around to see if anyone else was on the street. She could always scream for help if things turned ugly.

Carragh continued his stride alongside her. "How was the wedding?"

He was making small talk, which was ridiculous.

"It was beautiful. Magical." It was even more ridiculous

she answered him. Still, thinking about her sister looking so happy made her feel a little bit better, given her situation. "Something you'll see..." She wafted her hand. "You're engaged."

"I'm not." His nostrils flared.

"Well, your father sure thinks you are."

"My father doesn't have a say in the matter."

"Does he know that?"

"We don't see eye to eye on a lot of things." This man was unbelievably cool for just being told death might be in the cards for either of them.

"If you're so different from your family, why aren't you walking away?"

"Could you walk away from your family?"

"If they killed people? Yes." She stopped short, peered up at him and tried to ignore the red tattoo mark on his neck. "Have you ever killed anyone?"

"Yes."

She threw up her arms. "And you wonder why I can't be with you." She did not just say that.

"So, you've thought about it."

She had. Often, despite the absurdity of such a notion. Head in the clouds—that's what Starr and Phee had always said about her. She had dreams and a full life in her head that she would live someday. It didn't involve someone who could end another's life.

He easily caught up with her march, but kept his face forward. "It was in self-defense, and may I remind you, twice now, I have stepped in between my family and yours."

Yours. Shakedown was her family—all of them, whether by blood or not.

"Family is important," he continued. "It's the one thing my father and I agree on. It's just complicated."

"Declan is supposedly family, so why make so much trouble for him?"

"He went rogue."

"Like you."

He shrugged.

"So, that's why he hates Declan? Stupid reason," she spat.

He didn't answer for several long minutes. But then he stopped, and she found herself stilling. Her gaze lifting to meet his eyes.

"My father doesn't hate anyone. He doesn't feel anything."

"Are you sure about that? He seems to feel quite strongly about a lot of things."

"If only that were true." He kicked a branch lying on the sidewalk. It was such a little boy move made by a grown man. "He's trying to retake his standing in Baltimore."

"Retake?"

"My grandfather once owned quite a bit of this city."

Owned. What a sinister word.

"But my father's greed took over. Played hardball a few too many times, and people formed other alliances."

"And you?"

"That's a conversation for another time."

She spun and stumbled a little, getting her heel caught in the sidewalk for what seemed like the umpteenth time.

"You know, we would get to your house a lot faster if you would just let Sean drive us."

"Me getting into a car with two strange men?"

"I'm not a stranger to you."

He wasn't. She knew far too much about him, even if all her knowledge of him could fit into her mirrored compact. There also was something dark and familiar about him, and she didn't trust it—the longing, the desire, the *pull* toward him.

He strode over to the car, which screeched to a halt. He rapped on the window and Sean lowered it.

Carragh leaned against the door frame. "Go back to my father's. Find out what you can. I'll meet up with you later."

Without a word, Sean got out, dipped his head Luna's way, and sauntered back up the sidewalk like he was out for an afternoon stroll.

"Do people always do what you tell them to?"

"Everyone but a certain dancer. Please, get in." He gestured to the car.

"I won't be ordered about."

"Me either."

"Well, that's one thing we have in common."

Crinkles formed around his eyes. "We have a lot in common."

"You're just saying that to sleep with me."

"No, though we would do very little sleeping."

She imagined they wouldn't—and she imagined a lot. Damn him and his seductive aura. A little part of her nearly started shaking with laughter. *Seductive aura.* But the words were created for him. He couldn't have blended into a crowd if he tried—especially if said crowd was female.

She shook her head as if disgusted with herself and rounded the car. After she secured herself in the passenger seat, he lowered himself behind the steering wheel.

"Thank you," he said quietly.

She tried to keep her eyes straight ahead, but they kept darting to his profile.

It wasn't that Carragh was just classically handsome—the perfect Roman nose, the jawline, the gifted mop of black hair. It was that his presence was just so big and commanding. It demanded you look at him.

She sucked in a long breath and willed her attention to

the scenery. He was taking the long way, through tree-lined streets and not the highway.

The neighborhoods were familiar. She and her sisters had driven along these very roads, dreaming about how someday they might have a big house and big families. Now, Starr was on her way. Phoenix, however? She would find her own way with Declan.

A sadness crept up on her. Blanketed her whole body. Threatened to smother her. Today was a happy day, and the thick clouds of sadness that settled around her would not do.

She had a good life dancing. She loved Shakedown and all the people there. It's just every time she and her sisters got two steps forward it seemed there was someone ready to push them back three… or thirty. Men like Tomas MacKenna seemed born to threaten them.

When Carragh finally pulled into the parking lot of her apartment building, her body had numbed. He switched off the ignition and they both sat there, not moving to get out. He gripped the steering wheel with one hand and squeezed it.

"You strike me as a guy who would want to make sure I make it all the way in." What was she saying? She should not be encouraging this man.

His blue eyes focused on her. "You told me to stay away."

"I did."

She had to break this trance she'd fallen into, so she forced herself to open the door. Colder air wafted in and a chill ran through her whole body.

His hand descended on hers before she could move to get out, and she paused. "The reason I keep showing up is to watch over you. If you see anything disconcerting—anything at all, you call me." He held out an old-fashioned business card, stiff white paper with embossed silver letters.

Like the fool she was growing accustomed to being, she took it.

"But I will stay away… because you asked me to," he said.

"Good." It was the right thing to do—for both of them.

Once inside, she should have marched herself straight to the bathtub to wash off any remnants of that man's hands on her shoving her in a car. Put on music to drown out the remembered greasy voice of Tomas MacKenna. Put on a movie to ogle another man—any man—other than Carragh's face that seemed to have taken permanent residence in her mind.

Instead, she went to the window, parted the curtains with fingertips, and studied his car idling below. She couldn't see him, but she could see his large hand still curled around the steering wheel.

Finally, the car began to back up. Somehow, she knew he meant it when he said he'd stay away, and it made her stupidly, unjustifiably sad.

8

———

The chain rattled as Carragh's glove hit the bag. His shoulder ached and his hands were nearly numb, but no matter how he tried, he couldn't seem to hit it hard enough. He took more swings and picked up the pace.

"Who are you picturing?"

He rounded on Sean, whose telltale keys jangling by his side must have mixed with the chain's rattle.

The guy stepped back, arms up in surrender. "Whoa. By the look in your eyes right now, I'd say the guy's already dead."

Carragh grabbed the release tab with his teeth and freed his hand. "Maybe." He worked his fingers for a few minutes, then freed his other hand.

Sean casually widened his stance.

"Scaring you?" Carragh picked up his shirt, swiped under his arms, then threw it in the corner of his office. He'd grab a shower in a bit.

Sean didn't answer, of course. Carragh sniffed and grasped his tumbler of vodka sitting on his desk and threw it back. He then pounded to the bar cart to pour himself another. He took a sip and paused to glance outside. Bright sunshine lit up the water thirty floors below making it look like liquid blue fire—like a certain dancer's eyes.

"Drinking while working out. I like it." Sean plopped himself down on the gray linen couch and propped his feet up on his glass coffee table.

"Aren't you in Philadelphia?" He sipped his drink, kept his eyes on the scene below.

A train looking like a child's toy from this distance snaked along the tracks and then disappeared into a hole in the ground as if the ground had swallowed it.

The man didn't answer, so he turned to him. "Well?"

"Nothing to find. Your father's gonna be pissed. He rather looked forward to the leverage when the deal got signed."

"He usually does." So, the Monroes hadn't been talking smack about them like he suspected. His father seriously might be losing it.

Then again, how would he know? He'd been avoiding his father of late, leaving the dirty groundwork to Sean. Carragh was done being Tomas MacKenna's clean-up man.

"So, it's Friday." Sean stretched his arm across the back of his sofa. "Hot date, or you heading to Shakedown?"

The man was fishing. "You're not going to Shakedown." Carragh had already had to forcibly remove him one night— and he would continue to if he insisted on frequenting the place.

"You know there are ways to sneak around," the man chuckled. "You been doing it since you were 14."

"I don't need to sneak around."

"That why you haven't been to Declan's club in a while?"

It had been weeks since he'd laid eyes on Luna Belle. She'd told him to stay away, so he did despite it almost killing him. Her request only grew his desire to see her, drink in her pink lips and long legs.

He'd find himself heading south, the direction of Shakedown, when he shouldn't be. Or he'd see a woman with red hair and his hand would spin his steering wheel so he'd grow closer just to check to see if it was her. He'd once, absentmindedly, found himself scrolling through some God-awful burlesque videos on YouTube, seeking out a tall woman with hair the color of fire coral.

All of that only underscored the definite need to stay away. Obsessions were weaknesses—one he wasn't about to adopt.

Plus, his father was many things, but a liar was not one. He'd laid down the law that day he'd kidnapped her. It didn't mean Carragh was marrying some princess from one of the big families in the area, though.

"Saw Maura leaving," Sean yawned. "Thought you were through with her."

"Yeah, but she showed up. Dropped to her knees and opened her mouth."

"Then you should be in a better mood."

"She's not. Told her to leave." The thought of another woman's mouth on him right now made his stomach roil.

Sean appeared thoughtful. "Let's say we go get a real drink somewhere. Like on the waterfront?"

"Don't like my selections here?"

"Well, since you aren't offering any. Come on." He rose. "Let's swing by Shakedown. Tired of seeing your grumpy ass sulking so much. You're always in a better mood after you see her."

"I don't know what you're talking about. And no thanks." He wasn't jeopardizing her safety—and needed his father to think he won something. He hadn't. Carragh was merely buying time.

Now, though? Someone was putting grist to the rumor mill.

Just last week George Mack at the 219 Club had asked him what he knew about the waterfront. No one knew Carragh had just signed a deal with another developer known for understanding structures near bodies of water. He'd wanted to wait to announce in April, but someone talked as George referenced the developer by name.

Then there was James McFoy asking too many questions about what he planned for his future.

The real kicker was Tracy Blackstone, a commercial real estate agent, showing up at his office, cold, to lay out four properties for sale on the river.

"If you could just fuck her, get her—"

Carragh's arm pressed against the man's windpipe, his other hand circling the back of his neck. He'd moved so quickly Sean hadn't had time to suck in a breath after his bullshit words. He gasped a little.

"Maybe you *do* want to be on the other end of my boxing glove." His knee dented the couch, his leg pressed again his cousin's. The man shook, which was the right reaction.

"No time," Sean gasped out. "Got to go to Emerson's. Signing party."

Shit. Despite his father's suspicions, the MacKennas and Monroes were finally signing their joint deal—something in the making for a decade. Time really had slipped on him.

Carragh dropped his hold and Sean coughed as he bent over to place his hands on his legs. "Warn a guy before you go all caveman," he said to the floor.

"Watch your mouth in the future. You know the way out. See you there."

He and Sean had been beating the shit out of each other since kids so no hard feelings. Now, Carragh needed the man to go. He had to gather his thoughts since the vodka nor workout did little to right his mind. He'd grab a shower and then head over to the meeting or whatever his father wanted to call the display.

For years, the Monroes and MacKennas danced around one another in the same business. A shrinking number of shipping yards were where the two families finally realized working together might be in both of their best interests. The Monroes had the yards. The MacKennas had the goods —any goods with little paperwork required. A win-win for two families with similar and absent scruples.

And, they had about the same level of trust with one another, too.

His cousin's last-ditch effort—directed by Carragh's father—to see if the rumor Patrick Monroe was working a side deal yielded nothing. Kind of late in the game for seeking dirt, but his father's actions underscored how little confidence he had in anyone. Still, the partnership was being formalized.

Acquiring burlesque clubs wasn't high on the acquisition list—until they now were, thanks to Carragh's one mistake. He'd let people see he cared about the club and its inhabitants, a true weakness if his father ever saw one. Caring about anything wasn't on his father's to-do list any time soon, and Carragh was supposed to fall in those same callous footsteps.

He also was supposed to do business like his father.

Tomas went for the easy money—guns, contraband pharmaceuticals, whatever the black market demanded. Carragh, however, wanted a more survivable line of business.

The waterfront could be so much more than ingress and egress for Tomas' import business that didn't mind what came or went. Real, legitimate money could be made in importing industrial machinery—power generating, transport, medical, and more. Keeping the lights on and things moving was always in demand, and it was something

Carragh was going to see the MacKennas move into once his father retired for good.

Sean rose, stretched his neck and then faced him. "Need time to put on the brave face?"

"I have no other face." He had one—the one that ensured his father or anyone else never suspected he was more than through with his father's way of life.

Sean strode to the door, paused and gripped the frame. "Well, prepare yourself. Nicole will be there tonight."

Fucking great.

9

Emerson's was an old tourist-trap restaurant that had seen better days with its wooden bar smelling of stale beer, round tables with red-and-white-checked tablecloths, and dim, dark lighting. It also was an establishment that anyone with a conscience didn't frequent.

For business gatherings, Carragh's father favored the private room tucked in the back, probably due to its two-way mirror lining the side wall where he could look out over the restaurant and see whoever entered—but no one could see in.

Several sets of French doors led to a balcony whose bonus feature included a long staircase leading to the alley, should anyone not wish to be seen coming in or out of the place. Carragh had used it a time or two himself.

Tonight, however, he paraded through the front door. If he had to be here, let everyone in the restaurant see him and be signaled as to who was in back tonight. His presence alone would send enough tongues wagging—and it threw yet another bone to his father, who appreciated bold gestures.

The man was about to find out how bold he could be.

In the back room, his father stood with Patrick Monroe in the corner. They each held Scotches in their hand, and by the sound of their boisterous laughing, some story was being told.

Tita Monroe, Patrick's wife, chatted with two other women he didn't recognize, but who could tell them apart? They all sported the usual blond dye job done up in a French twist and had diamonds hanging from their earlobes.

There were at least eight other people in the room, mostly men, some who Carragh recognized as muscle, others whose identity was a complete unknown. But then he'd stayed out of the family's tentative alliance with the Monroes. It made it easier to make the deal null and void once he was in charge.

Nicole was conspicuously absent given her trophy daughter status with her family. They trotted her out when they wanted to distract the men in the room. She'd make her preferred grand entrance later. She'd also know Carragh himself would show up late on purpose. Then again, the woman knew too much about him.

He'd unwisely unloaded on her one night after a fuckfest in his father's limousine two years ago—how he hated being his father's lackey. She'd cooed and agreed he was meant for bigger things. A snow job if he ever heard one.

"Ah, so he does lift his head from paperwork." A slap to his shoulder and the clink of ice in a glass had him turn around.

Carragh held out his hand. "Leo. Please tell me that's Midleton?" He eyed the man's glass.

The man chuffed. "Thought you were a vodka man."

"Changing flavors."

Leo pressed his lips together and nodded slowly. "Heard

that. Let's get you a drink." He inclined his head to the bar. A cute little brunette in a black vest and starched white shirt smiled as they neared.

"Get my man a Midleton, will ya, gorgeous?"

She dipped her head and fluttered her eyelashes up and down at Carragh. When had women grown so obvious?

Leo swirled the liquid in his glass. "So… heard you might be changing a lot of things soon."

"Don't believe everything you hear, Leo."

As the girl poured his drink, Leo leaned in. "So, this deal with the Monroes. How do you feel about it?"

"Carragh." His father's voice boomed, his hand held up in a come hither gesture.

He leaned down to Leo. "Come see me tomorrow." He knew Leo to be very unhappy with his father—though the man's loyalty had proved meager to anyone over the years. Carragh could still get information out of him without revealing his own—like why he thought Carragh might be changing things.

He took the whiskey the girl set on the bar top. "Thanks…" he glanced at her name tag "…Susan." He dropped a twenty into her empty tip jar.

"Patrick, you remember my eldest." Tomas put his hand on Carragh's shoulder.

Carragh took Patrick's outstretched hand. "Patrick."

The man's eyes dimmed a bit at the informality. It felt fucking great.

"Carragh. You look like the spitting image of your mother." A smile returned to his eyes and his face in record time. He recovered well—comparing him to the maternal side of the family over the paternal. Carragh had to give him a point for that.

"So they say." He took a sip of the whiskey.

Patrick eyed his glass. "Thought you were a vodka man."

"Didn't know my choice of drink was so well-documented."

Tomas studied the ice in his glass. "Carragh enjoys change. It's why he'll be a terrific asset in our Philly operation."

Philadelphia? Like hell. It was so like his father to spring orders on him in a public place. "We'll see. If you'll excuse me, I'm going to get some air."

Carragh made his way to the first set of French doors and stepped out into the warm night air. March was such a crapshoot in Maryland—snow could be falling from the sky or the sun could be warming daffodils.

Just the thought of the flower raised an image of his mother. It was her favorite.

"Carragh MacKenna." Nicole's voice sounded from the other end of the balcony. She leaned against the banister, a cigarette in her hand, black hair hung loose, her long waves flowing over her shoulders.

She pitched the cigarette over the side and pushed off. Her breasts wobbled underneath her wrap dress as she moved to him in her heels.

He met her in the center of the balcony so they'd be hidden behind the brick wall between the two doors. No reason to get anyone's tongues wagging more than they already were.

Her heel seemed to give way and she tumbled forward. He caught her, and a flash of Luna losing her balance a few weeks ago crossed his brain.

"Oh, clumsy me." She clung to his forearm. "Ooo, it's so cold out, and you're so warm."

He set his drink on the railing and shrugged off his coat, draping it around her shoulders.

"True gentleman. Thank you." She took his drink, took a swig. "Mmm. Whiskey. Not your usual." Her dark, almond eyes shone like amber. She was beautiful. She also was a pain in the ass.

"That's what I keep hearing."

She handed him the glass, now marked with her lip print. "Where have you been keeping yourself, Carragh MacKenna?"

"I've been around." He sniffed. Her perfume invaded his nostrils.

"I was beginning to think you didn't like me anymore."

"You're an easy woman to like, Nicole."

"Like but not love?"

Here they went. "I'm sure many men are in love with you."

"They are. But none are…" she placed her hand on his pec and looked up at him "…you. I could love you, you know."

Could. Interesting choice of words.

"You know how well…" she trailed her manicured fingers down his chest to his belt buckle "…I love." She licked her lips and began to bend down to her knees.

This woman's mouth was familiar—too familiar. Two years ago, he'd have thrust his cock down her throat until he was spent even with people a few feet away. Two years ago, his head wasn't full of a certain dancer with her delicious-looking, pink lips, however.

He grasped her wrists and pulled her up. "Another time."

Lines around her eyes deepened. "There may not be another time."

"My loss then."

"Yes, it is. In more ways than one. Or perhaps I should die my hair… red?" She arched an eyebrow.

A muscle twitched in his eye. "Look, Nicole—"

"You're a fool, Carragh MacKenna. Dallying with strippers is one thing. But you think they're…" she tossed her chin in the air and toward the crowd inside "…just going to let you walk away?"

"I don't walk."

She smirked and breached the last bit of space between them. "Let me rephrase." She batted her eyelashes up at him. "Or let you take over?"

His gut twisted. Perhaps he'd underestimated Nicole's intelligence or observation skills. Someone wasn't just talking about him. Someone was putting two-and-two together and coming up with things he'd barely voiced.

She leaned forward, rolled her bottom lip into her teeth, and let it go with a smack. "Oh, I know all about your little obsession with a certain redhead. But you'd be wise to choose someone more intelligent to sit next to you on your throne—someone who knows the family business."

"I already know the family business."

"Ah, but do they…" she inclined her head once more toward the inside room "…know what business you're cooking up? Do they know how much time you spend down at the waterfront?"

"You don't know what you're talking about." That damned muscle twitched in his eye again. In addition to his plans, too many people also kept bringing up Shakedown for his taste.

"Whatever you say, Carragh."

She lifted his jacket off her shoulders and let it fall to the ground. "Thanks for keeping me warm. For a bit."

She was right about one thing. He had been a fool. One, for ever letting this woman near his cock, and two, for letting *anyone* know of his plans. Three people had been told, which meant he had three mouths to now cap: Declan, who knew by accident, Petra, who knew by merely being present to his phone calls, and more recently, Sean, who knew by pushing Carragh into a corner.

He grabbed his jacket and jogged down the back steps. He wasn't going another night to find out who the hell was trying to force his hand. He'd start with the obvious person first—the one who hated his guts.

10

Luna fingered the oval silver locket, the size of a small clamshell. "Are you sure you found this in... that?" She pointed to the musty old army-green jacket that he'd worn constantly the last time few times she'd seen him—that is, before he'd become so bedridden.

"Yes. Look inside," Maven urged.

Luna cracked it open and found two photographs, one on each side. The man pictured on the left wasn't even looking into the camera. But on the other side, the spitting image of her mother smiled back at her.

She glanced at her father who lay asleep in the big hospital bed, so shriveled he was nearly swallowed by a checkered blanket. The man in the picture *could* be him.

She'd like to have asked him about this strange finding, but he didn't recognize her and was now slumbering and maybe dreaming of times lost inside his head.

Maven touched her arm. "I'm not allowed to say much around the patients here, but you and your sisters may want to come visit a bit more often. I mean..." She glanced down at Luna's father, pity crossing her features at seeing the man who'd shrunk to half his size from when Luna had lived with him, seventeen long years ago.

"He doesn't have much time left?"

"I have been working with people dealing with Alzheimer's my whole life, honey. And I know when they've had enough themselves, if you know what I mean. They tend to… choose."

Choose when to die. What a thought. "Thanks for calling me. And for this." She lifted the locket and silver chain it was affixed to.

"I knew right away that woman inside is your momma, isn't it?"

"It is." She tucked the item in her purse, which clinked against her phone. That only reminded her she had to meet her sisters soon.

At least being summoned to her father's bedside gave her something to occupy the first half of her day. She'd had too much time lately to think, to muse about the stupidest things. She should be running choreography in her head or planning the grocery shopping. Instead, her mind drifted to imaging what Carragh MacKenna was up to.

His sudden disappearance, even if she had demanded it, felt odd. No limo sightings, no blue eyes shining at her from the darkened audience.

"Well, you all visit anytime." She patted Luna's back. "We don't pay much mind to visiting hours. Just come when the mood strikes."

She might stop by, but Starr and Phee? They'd visit when hell was a frozen tundra. Her sisters had said their piece long ago. She, however, had little to say. Rather, she had *questions.*

Did he love them—truly? And why did he leave her relatively alone but focus most of his rages on her sisters? And why had he kissed her on the cheek at child protective services but not Starr? That last one had bothered her her whole life.

Starr didn't seem to remember much about that day he left them with strangers. She seemed to think he dropped them off. He hadn't. She remembered every detail as clear as the man who now dented a hospital bed.

Phee was in the hospital, the event that led to Child Protective Services showing up at their doorstep. They announced in a hushed voice that Phee would live. Starr's eyes could have driven nails into their father's back at that moment. They didn't know she'd been in danger of dying.

He'd gripped the door frame with his beefy hand, sweat stains forming a long oval down the side of his shirt—and nodded slowly. He then pushed the door open for them to step inside.

Them. Two men and an elderly woman with an annoying sing-song voice crouched down to Starr, who had stayed standing. Luna had cowered by the couch. A cold terror had gripped her heart and her legs shook.

There was no coaxing her to come forward. One of the men simply reached down and lifted her into his arms. She hadn't even fought it, though he smelled funny and his face was a stone mask of nonchalance.

Their father, in that beat-up tan sedan, had followed the car that drove them to the government office. He then had taken Luna by the shoulders, stared down at her with red-rimmed eyes that held a misery she'd not seen before. She peered up at him, wanting to know what was going on, what was he doing? Letting these strangers take them?

For the next few days, as she and Starr stayed in some family's attic room that smelled of sawdust and mothballs, she'd honestly believed he'd be back for them. He never did return.

"Dad?" she asked the sleeping man.

He didn't stir. She needed to go anyway.

The hallway, which resembled more of a hospital than any other place he'd been placed, was still. A man dozed in a wheelchair down the hallway, and a nurse pushed open a door with her butt and disappeared further down. So, this is where the forgotten go in their final days.

Thank God she had her sisters. Not having anyone in your life had to be truly awful.

It made her think of Carragh. He had a big family and yet seemed to have no one, in an odd way.

She blasted the air conditioning for a few minutes, just to clear her head, and pulled out of the parking lot.

What did Carragh do at night? Did he live alone? Or did he bring a different woman home every night just to keep the sheets warm?

She got so mired into thinking about him, she pulled into the parking lot of the Phoenix Rising Dance Studio, not even realizing how she'd gotten there.

She hoofed it inside to find Naomi and Starr at the near end of the ballroom space, bantering about something. Behind them, two girls were fanning out the parachute silk as if readying themselves for an aerial practice over a round crash mat.

Naomi raised an eyebrow. "I think she can do it."

"Ten bucks says he gives her a credit only." Starr held up her fist.

"You're on." They fist-bumped.

Starr turned to her. "L., want in on the bet? Phee wants to return forty-two costumes that her seven-year-olds have already grown out of before the performance."

"Good luck with that one."

"Hey," Naomi called to a girl who had climbed even higher on the silks. "Be careful." She jogged over and grasped the silk ends.

"My," Starr whispered under her breath to Luna. "Naomi certainly has taken to her role seriously."

It was a far cry from her stripper days from which Phee had rescued her. That horrible Maxim's place where she and her sisters also had escaped from. Even there, Phoenix had taken more abuse than she had.

Phee strutted in, waving her phone. "Done and done. Naomi, package them up."

"Get out." Starr's mouth dropped to an 'O.'

Naomi flounced back to them and held out her hand for her winnings from Starr.

Luna dropped her purse in a chair on the side wall and herself in the other one.

"What's up with you?" Starr frowned.

"Just came back from seeing Dad."

Phee frowned at her. "Please don't spoil my great day. I have news that matters."

Naomi pointed to the back storeroom. "That's my cue."

After Naomi disappeared, Luna turned to her sisters. "You need to know he probably doesn't have much time left."

Phee held up her hand to stop any more words from *spoiling her day.*

"So, what's your news?" Just dropping her visit would be the wisest course of action. Sharing anything about their father only raised their familiar anger regarding their past with him. There would be time later to share the locket with them.

"Well, it's more like a decision. I already told Starr. It's time for me to stop dancing onstage. In fact, I haven't for the last couple of weeks, and honestly, I don't miss it at all."

"I wasn't surprised to hear this." Starr smiled at her. "You're an awesome teacher."

Phee appeared thoughtful. "I am."

Oddly, Luna was shocked to learn of this development.

"But… your acts?" Phee's matador act was one of the most popular at Shakedown, and they had several new group routines that had gone over so well in the last year.

"You don't need me for them. I'm going to teach full-time. And then there will be a new dancer pool."

Luna sucked in a long breath. "And this will truly make you happy?"

"Are you kidding? I own a dance studio." She spread her arms wide. "Well, partly own. But yes."

"Then that's what you need to do." Luna was happy for her sister, honestly. It's just she didn't think changes would happen so suddenly. But then she was the one to insert their father back into their lives. She hadn't meant for it to get so messy.

"Wow, things have really changed in the last year, haven't they?" Luna asked.

"Mostly for the better, I'd say." Phee wasn't normally this optimistic.

Starr pulled her sisters closer. "Well, why not make it a good news day all around? It's still really early yet, but…" Starr took a hand of each of them and placed them over her belly "…you two are going to be aunts. Due around Christmas." She cocked her head back and forth. "Or thereabouts. I must have gotten pregnant before we even got married."

Luna's jaw fell open. "Wow. Oh, my God. I can't believe it." She placed her other hand on Starr's stomach. "A baby." She bounced up and down in place.

"I know, right. Can you imagine? Me? A mother?"

Phee's eyes misted and she hugged Starr tight. "You're going to be the best mom."

"Let me in there." Luna wrapped her arms around them, her nose full of Phee's cinnamon scent. A little boy or girl? Or maybe twins—one boy and one girl. That would be the best because then she could buy any baby clothes that looked cute.

She broke the huddle first. "Hold up. When will Momma Cherry know?"

Phee laughed a little. "I'm going to need earplugs to block out the excited screaming for that day."

"Dibs on first babysitting duty." Luna held up her hand. "If I don't get it in now, Momma is going to swoop in… oh, and I'm in charge of her wardrobe." Luna would like nothing more than a baby to cuddle and spoil and love with all her heart.

"So sure it'll be a girl?" Phee scoffed.

"Or his wardrobe. Or maybe twins." She bobbed her head up and down at Starr's shocked face. "Now, what are the nursery colors?"

"It's a little soon for that."

"Never. All the rage is to have neutral colors—not sway the gender thing."

Phee raised both her eyebrows and glanced around. "Wait a minute. You're pregnant and Nathan let you leave the house without him?"

Luna burst out laughing. And it felt so damned good. When was the last time she laughed?

Sure, nothing truly would ever be the same again. Starr probably was not far behind Phee when it came to leaving her performance days behind. But a baby would be so much better! Her mind swam with little outfits she could buy, and chubby arms and legs, and little baby giggles.

"You're right, Luna. So much change." Starr grasped both her sisters' hands once more.

This last year had seen a seismic shift in their lives—and now, even more would come.

"One thing hasn't changed," she said.

"Sisters forever. Friends always," they said in unison.

Her good feelings stayed with her until she got back in her car to head to Shakedown. Phee and Starr were now settled, their futures stretching out before them like a paved road. It's what she'd always wanted—stability for all three of them. Now, two were settled.

As for her? She had no idea what her future had in store. That was the only thing that was really unsettling her, to not really know where her life would go, how it would end up.

When her mother died, she left fond memories. When her father died, he'd leave nothing behind but misery. And when she died? What would she have left? She'd be some distant memory of a good time someone once had when visiting a burlesque club. Not much of a legacy.

Her thoughts drifted to Carragh—a man where family meant something, even if it was twisted and dark.

She hadn't seen him for three weeks and two days—a time frame she really needed to stop counting already. He was staying away as requested. Yet somehow, it felt worse when he wasn't there. The club had seemed… quiet, too quiet.

Phee would say his absence was worse because the most dangerous snakes were those you couldn't see.

Starr would say it was because he was off making plans for the MacKennas' next assault.

Neither was wrong.

But Carragh wasn't a snake or a soldier. He was something entirely else—an enigma that she couldn't stop trying to decipher.

She reached into her purse and pulled out the locket. At a red light, she slipped it over her head. Maybe someday she'd pass it down to her own daughter—if she ever got so lucky to have her own family. If she did, it couldn't be with someone who was tied to violence—even if he lured her like a Venus flytrap. She'd had enough of that in her lifetime.

She pulled into the Shakedown parking lot just as Cortelana and Sally Mae were doing the same. She waved to her fellow dancers as she popped her trunk. She reached in and pulled out her garment bag holding her blue velvet dress, her Steamboat Sally sailor outfit, and another duffel bag filled with panties, cheap satin gloves, and other little items that really needed a good soak in a gentle washing cycle. Living alone meant one good thing—having the washing machine to yourself.

She pushed open the bright pink makeup room door and found Cherry in a full-on tizzy.

"Emergency. Crisis. Defcon one." Cherry was picking items out of a large canvas makeup bag with *Life Can Be Beautiful. Can You Be?* etched on the side.

Nicholas/Nikki had slunk behind his makeup counter after giving Luna a big wide-eyed "Don't ask me" look. Aspen was rummaging through a big trunk in the back of the room. "None in here," she called.

Luna dropped the duffel bag at her makeup station. "What's wrong?"

"I cannot find my eyelash glue and I have thirty minutes before these have got to be *on*." Cherry fanned her large brown eyes. "Oh, no. Do you think the drug store down the street has any? I could get Max to run out." She rustled through the big drawer in her makeup stand.

After hooking her garment bag on her stand, Luna grabbed her makeup bag and tossed it at her. "Use mine."

"You know it has to be latex-free." She whispered the last two words.

"I have both in there."

Cherry unzipped the bag and within seconds pulled out

the tiny tube of latex-free glue, pinched between her two long red fingernails.

"Oh, thank all the goddesses. The night has been saved," she called out loudly and lifted the tiny tub toward a smiling Aspen. "Momma Cherry does not go on without her eyelashes."

Luna pecked her on the cheek.

"Careful." She sang. "I'm moisturized, shaded, and contoured."

"And beautiful."

She popped open the clear eyelash box and lifted one of the falsies with her fingernail. "You say that to all your drag mothers." She unscrewed the tiny top of the glue tube and put a drop on the end of a toothpick.

Luna's eyes stung—out of the blue, for totally no reason whatsoever. She had to get a move on herself. She unzipped the bag and went to work organizing her outfits for the night. She had at least five acts to do, and there'd be no time in between to dally.

As Cherry applied her eyelashes, she glanced over at Luna in the mirror. "So. What do you think?" Her voice had lowered.

"They look good to me."

"No, love." She swiveled her stool to face Luna. *"Phoenix.* Retiring." She glanced around at Aspen, who wasn't paying any attention to them. Cortelana and Sally Mae strode in, laughing. "I was going to bring it up later, but you know how patient I am *not."*

"It was only a matter of time. She could use the break." Luna clicked on the lights on her mirror.

Cherry scooted her chair closer and grasped both her wrists. "When I got the call today, well, I just couldn't believe it. The Shakedown stage without Phoenix Rising." She placed a hand against her chest. "Well, I just can't go there... I thought it was just a phase."

"I'd say teaching 100 people a month is more than that." Phee really had taken to being the teacher over the performer. Regular classes and special workshops kept her busier than ever because Luna honestly had never seen her sister so happy. It was like she found her place.

"I know." Cherry pursed her lips together and pulled a tissue from the box sitting on Luna's stand. She sniffed and brought it to her nose. "It's just the end of an era I was not prepared for. But..." She straightened and slapped the makeup counter with her palm. "If you're happy, I'm happy." She lowered her voice and glanced around the mirror at Aspen, who still wasn't paying them any attention. "I might even offer my skills to her studio. Someone out there is dying to learn to drag from Momma Cherry's wisdom."

Nicholas/Nikki poked his head around the make-up stand. "Great idea."

"You can be my assistant." Cherry pointed at her fellow performer.

Honestly, it was an idea she'd love for Cherry to focus on. Luna did not want to get into either of her sisters' plans tonight. Clearly, Cherry had heard about Phee but not Starr's pregnancy. Luna would not be the one to spill the baby beans. She had to focus on tonight and think about all the changes happening tomorrow.

Cherry blinked at her expectedly. "You sure you're alright?"

"Of course. Why wouldn't I be?" She laid out all her make-up for the night: foundation, concealer, contouring cream, eye shadow, three kinds of liner, her own preferred eyelash glue, eyelashes, and... where was that eyelash curler?

"It certainly is the end of an era." She swiveled back to focus on her second eyelash. "And Starr taking nights off. It's not like that girl. Don't let them abuse your good nature, kitten."

"You don't have to worry about us."

"Well, the O'Malley sisters will never be parted, but it looks like you're going to Diana Ross them soon and make yourself the star you were born to be." She fluttered her eyes to the ceiling.

"We're all stars at Shakedown." She didn't want to keep talking about this. It made her oddly tired.

"You always were the romantic one, Miss Luna Belle." Cherry winked at her." And reliable."

Was she?

She dabbed some foundation on the back of her hand and went to work putting on the Luna Belle face. With an applicator, she dabbed and spread the makeup over her skin— something she'd done five nights a week for almost seven years. She could run through these steps in her sleep. Maybe that's why Phoenix was done, and Starr was beginning to show signs of the same.

How long could Luna keep up? Keep applying the same shade of Ben Nye foundation—Ingenue mixed with Geisha? Or stop at the drug store every other week for more eyelash glue? Hand-wash her beaded costumes?

Honestly? A lot longer because she loved dancing. She'd just hoped she'd do it with her sisters for many more years. She was happy for them, but Cherry had it right. End of an era summed up their situation perfectly.

She moved to contouring her cheekbones, her arm weighted heavy. Normally, she'd get a jolt of energy knowing she was about to go on. Today was too busy, that was all. The usual adrenaline spike five minutes before taking the stage would come.

11

___

Carragh took another sip of the port; not his usual drink, but Declan had never offered anything to him before. He chalked it up to good manners as the man had an open bottle on his desk. "You do know it's in your best interest to keep this meeting under wraps."

Declan swiveled in his desk chair. "I never asked to see you. Why would I tell anyone?"

True, he'd forced his way inside, telling the man he was there to warn him. Declan had protested, but the glimmer of interest in his eyes was enough for Carragh to press for a closed-door meeting.

Declan tapped his armrest. "You here to warn me the police might find yet another guy face-first in the water not 300 yards from here? Or more drugs being potentially planted in my car?"

Carragh could say the two were unrelated, but he might be guessing. "I don't know anything about either of those." He truly didn't.

"Then what do you know?"

"First, I'm going to tell you something in good faith." He

opened both palms. "I trust you'll keep it under your hat. I bought that warehouse down the street." It cost him a pretty penny—six million—but it was worth it for his father not to have it. Plus, he'd needed Declan to trust him to reveal his own secrets, like how he might have been working against him more actively than he'd have first guessed.

Declan's nostrils flared. "Planning on opening up your own import-export?"

"I don't know what I'm going do with it, but I didn't want my father to have it. Just like you, I don't want him to have this club." More truth tumbled from his lips. Why not continue the trend?

"Don't patronize me." His incessant rocking of his chair stilled. "You want to start your own operation."

"I do, but it doesn't have to be what my father was into. Diversification, Declan. You should try it sometime."

He had bought property up and down the waterfront to throw a monkey wrench into his father's plans—but it could come in handy for his own ideas for import-export later.

If Carragh knew anything about his father, it was the man wasn't a thinker. He was more muscle and bluster. If he discovered a Starboard Enterprises bought some property, it'd never occur to him to ask who was behind it. If he did? So what? Carragh would simply claim the property was going to be a gift to the man later. It was a gift he would never deliver, but what would the man know?

In the meantime, Carragh worked on setting up his own alliances. Sean wasn't fully "in" on the plans yet, and Carragh wasn't sure he ever would be. His cousin was suspicious of him? He was growing the same of Sean.

"So, what are you planning?" Skepticism swam in Declan's eyes.

"How much do you want to know?"

"Not sure I want to know anything. Just want you to keep it out of my club."

"I may not be able to do that." His father, if he couldn't have Declan join the family firm, would try to ruin him. "If you let me help you, trusted me—"

"And why would I do that? You shot your own brother."

"To save who you care about." He raked his fingers through his hair. Dammit, this wasn't how he wanted this conversation to go. Declan may not believe he was a MacKenna but he sure had the stubborn streak of most of the males in his family. He also was smart. Not many people turned the tables on him.

"Take yourself out." Declan rose. "We've got nothing else to discuss."

He rose. He knew when a meeting was over. "I'm going to stick around. Watch the show."

"Carragh." His warning tone really irritated. "I meant what I said. Stay away from Luna."

Funny how people kept telling him that. "You know how well telling me what to do works."

"She doesn't want you."

His gut twisted unexpectedly. "That what she said?"

Neither of them had to name Luna to know exactly who they referenced.

Declan slanted his eyes up at him. "What do you know? You do care about her."

He shrugged. So, the man had seen something in his eyes. He was damned sick of hiding his interest anyway.

"Why?"

"Why are you with Phoenix?"

"None of your goddamned business."

"My thoughts exactly." He couldn't articulate why he couldn't stay away from Luna.

Declan's voice stopped him at the door. "Ask yourself this.

Is she safer with you or without you? That's the only question you should be asking if you care about her at all."

Fair point. "With me." He didn't know shit about that, really, but he was damned sick of being told what to do around the woman. "Keep vigilant, Declan. My father's not one to let a loss go unpunished."

Which was another reason he could shoehorn into his box of reasons to stay close to Luna: he felt the need to keep watch on Shakedown—and her.

He tapped the door frame. "It'd be a shame to lose this place. If you'd sell, I would take care of everyone here."

"People don't convey like draperies."

"Yes, well… My offer to buy still stands."

"Still not selling."

He murmured. "Still taking in the show."

He headed out to the main floor, just in time to see a lithe redhead with perfect legs and lips he was dying to taste take the stage.

12

Luna stepped into the center of the oval spotlight. "If You Wear That Velvet Dress" by Jools Holland and Bono, her favorite song to dance to, had the audience hushed and reverent—just the way she liked it. It was like holding them in her hands.

Faint smoke curled in the beam of light and the tips of the ostrich feathers of her fan fluttered as she swept it down in a long arc. The tinkling piano sounds met with strings and Bono's voice and she pivoted in a three-point turn. Her belly didn't do its usual little flip when she executed the move in a perfect line.

Shapes moved in her periphery, and the flash of watches and rings cut through the darkened audience. They seemed so far away from her, like maybe she was behind glass.

As the song built, she began to show more leg through her long, blue velvet gown. But it was when she shimmied to the piano the audience broke their silence. A man whistled. Glasses clinked. Her shoe scraped on the stage under her feet. All ordinary sights and sounds on a Friday. Only tonight wasn't feeling like an ordinary night.

She twirled, pranced, and took long strides across the stage. She tried to hook into the music, but it wasn't coming for some reason.

Luna twirled, felt the soft brush of feathers against her bare arm. She lifted her knees high and her chin even higher. Soaked in the murmurs coming from the audience nearest the stage.

Her dance steps would never abandon her, and she knew how to dance through boredom. She had to do it now and again, but tonight she really didn't want to have to rely on her training. She wanted to feel good.

Three unfamiliar men by the stage gaped at her. She wafted the fans across their heads and one playfully batted the feathers away. Another whistled. More catcalls urged her on, but each kick and prance took a supreme effort, like moving through deep water.

Then the floor gave way. For a moment, her ankle had weakened, and she'd almost tripped.

She was so off her game.

Rough voices somewhere in the dark snapped her out of her thoughts. A fight had broken out. The silhouette of a huge man—likely Max—formed, roughly handling someone in the back.

She really wasn't fully present, was she? The emptiness of the stage pressed down on her, as if the open space really was under deep water.

She had danced solo hundreds of times in the seven years at Shakedown, but she'd never felt alone, or so detached onstage before, at least not until tonight. The reason for her unease was so obvious it was laughable. She and her two sisters would never dance again together, and Luna would be the last O'Malley sister to take a bow on this very stage sometime this year.

Declan appeared in back, supervising the throw-out of

whoever started the fight. That's when Luna saw him—his familiar shock of black hair and blue eyes aimed her way. Immediately, the heaviness that had taken residence in her chest lightened.

Luna waved her fans toward the audience, and they burst into applause. Declan angrily swiped at the curtains and disappeared. Carragh still stood in the back—staring at her, hard.

He stuffed his hands into his pockets and cocked his head a little. His regard was magnetic, and lethal to her focus.

He entered the room like a roll of thunder announcing a storm, and it thrilled her. A tug that began in her belly lowered to between her thighs.

She should be afraid of him, even hate him. Instead, Luna couldn't hate him if she tried. And therein lay yet another issue. She didn't know how to love her sisters and love him at the same time.

She shuddered at her thought. Love him? She couldn't. She barely knew the man.

He stepped down onto the main floor and moved closer.
Oh, God.
The storm was about to break.

His legs carried him further—straight to the lip of the stage. The night was almost over and there was one empty table, begging for his presence. He plunked his ass down and enjoyed the fire in her eyes—the fire with its dual message. *Fuck me and fuck off.*

Yeah, she would like to be unhappy to see him—but she wasn't.

He, however, was not ambivalent at drinking in her beauty. Sean was right. His mood instantly lightened at seeing her. One glance at her pink lips twisting down at him lit him up on the inside.

She cocked her ankle and jutted out a hip, the jangle of beads slapping against her thigh—a leg he'd love to grasp and yank open.

"Sir, what can I get you?" a waitress he didn't even glance at whispered near his ear. He wasn't taking his eyes off the stage.

"Vodka. Straight up. Grey Goose."

Luna's blue eyes glanced his way but quickly moved to the table behind him. So, she was having trouble ignoring him. He rather enjoyed stirring her up. She certainly did that to him.

Every aspect of her was an invitation to his cock as well as an instant problem. She had ahold of him. No one got ahold of him. Yet here he sat.

Women were a tangle of contradictions, but he'd never met one who created such a paradox in him.

Luna had no idea how interesting she was. She was soft and steel, sweet and spice. She was all that was pure and good but as tempting as the devil himself. He fucking loved the mismatches. Everyone in his world were cardboard cut-outs compared to the dancer who glared down at him.

She turned her back on him, which only presented her very fine ass that she shook with abandon. The things he would do to that flesh… One look at her and his mind and body, normally disciplined, ran amuck.

If she was his woman, he'd shower her with anything she desired—jewels, vacations, houses. Hell, he'd build Luna her own stage if she wanted. He'd do something good with that warehouse space. To hell with Declan and his warnings to stay away. He'd make anything happen for her.

A drink appeared on his table, and he grasped it just so he had something to curl his hand around.

When she pivoted and rolled her hips, he had a thought. *I will remember this time.* She onstage and he sitting a few feet away with his hands fisting a cut-glass tumbler that would leave patterns in his skin. He would remember this moment his whole life when anything was possible. It all lay ahead of them.

He'd yet to learn about her past life beyond the handful of tragedies he'd gotten privy to. He'd yet to memorize all her different kinds of laughs. He'd yet to lay her underneath him, find out if she liked her neck kissed or her nipples suckled—how hard and how soft. He'd yet to do so many things with her.

But he could. He could stay—or he could walk. The choice was his.

Yet, who was he kidding? It wouldn't be enough to just remember this night and its infinite possible endings. If the last few weeks were any indication, avoiding her didn't work. His only real option was to resume inching his way closer to having her.

A hand descended on his shoulder, and he nearly came out of his skin. Man, he must have been wholly mesmerized by Luna.

"So jumpy." Nicole's irritating voice cut into the air like a cockroach skittering across a hardwood floor.

She lowered herself to the empty chair near him, that pretentious fur coat dripping off one shoulder revealing a bright red spaghetti strap number that would have made a lingerie slip look like a Victorian dress in comparison. It was more than Luna wore onstage, but Nicole's presentation would make a man take her in the back alley, while Luna's would make a man book a suite at the Ritz.

He purposefully arched an eyebrow Nicole's way. "Slumming?" Why confirm this place had any value to him, though she likely already knew.

"Isn't that what you're doing?" She sent her gaze toward Luna, who was teasing a couple at the other end of the stage —still trying to ignore him, perhaps. "I really don't get what you see in her. I mean, I suppose she's pretty enough." Her tone dripped with feigned boredom. He knew better. Nicole hated competition.

He grasped her arm—hard—and yanked her to standing. "Let me call you a car."

She jerked free. "I have a car. What I don't have is any understanding why you're making things so difficult." She touched his pec, and he didn't hide his shudder from their proximity. "Carragh, love…"

"You're disrupting the show. And you haven't seen difficult, sweetheart."

He managed to get her up the aisle and back to the bar, hissing and squirming like the feral cat she was.

"Let me go, Carragh." She shrugged her coat back up over her and spit hair from her face which then softened as her eyes slanted. "I don't mind being manhandled so long as there's something in it for me. You up for it?"

This woman had no boundaries. "Where is your car?"

She smiled. "Now you're talking."

Like he was going to climb into her backseat like a teenager? "Home. Now."

She huffed but let him lead her out of Shakedown and into the parking lot where, sure enough, a familiar sedan and driver waited.

He opened the door for her and she pivoted on him. "I'll let my father know what a gentleman you are for getting me to my car."

"You do that." He could give a rip what Patrick Monroe thought of him.

But she did give him the perfect excuse to stay—to ensure Luna Belle got home okay. He didn't trust Nicole to not idle around the corner, waiting for an ambush on the woman he was now officially obsessed with. So what if Carragh didn't wait on women? He'd wait for the next century to turn for Luna. That fact came dangerously close to resembling a hostage situation, but he'd deal with that problem another time.

13

Luna pushed open the exit door. The parking lot's automatic light clicked on the second her heel hit the pavement and illuminated a man leaning against her car. If he were anyone else, she'd have scooted back inside and retrieved Max. She probably still should, given who stared at her.

She knew it was Carragh before she saw his face. The way his hand leaned on the hood of her car, the curls of black hair against his neck over that red tattoo mark were details she hadn't realized she'd memorized. Details she should try to forget.

The night air was cool on her skin as she moved closer. "Why are you here?"

"Checking on you." He pushed off.

"Because your fiancée caught you taking in a show?"

"She's not my fiancée. And how did you know who she was? Googling me?"

He wishes. "Lucky guess. I recognize a jealous woman when I see one. I see them a lot."

"She won't bother you again. I promise." He frowned.

"I can take care of myself. I don't need you to play white knight."

He stepped toward her. "Care for a drink then?"

Only when he moved had she realized she'd frozen. She shook herself free and reached into her purse for her keys. "What happened to Papa's orders?"

He took her keys from her hand, the jangle loud in the still night air. The brush of his fingertips blanked her mind, and a wave of pure aliveness swelled inside her.

"Grown men don't ask their fathers anything." He inserted the key in the lock and opened the door for her.

She threw her bag in the back seat. "I don't drink." She had to at least put up a fight.

"I wouldn't force anything on you."

"Wouldn't you?" She asked it too quickly. She'd filled the space between his question and her answer so fast a breath couldn't have fit in between.

His face registered he understood something, a truth she hadn't even wanted to admit to herself. She'd thought about him forcing her—Carragh grasping her wrists, pushing them behind her so he could press himself against her. His icy eyes capturing hers. He'd gauge her reaction, and then he'd take. And if he did, this was a man who didn't conquer. He *branded*.

He casually advanced on her—one small step that removed all polite space between them. Her body began to hum. Her heart galloped in her chest. With him this close, she felt she'd been plugged into an electrical box and was growing new nerve endings.

He'd changed her forever. He'd woken a primitive need and a raging lust inside her that, once he left, would simmer under her skin for hours. It would always be like with him, wouldn't it?

But worse? After he left she wouldn't be able to stop

thinking about *him* and who he was. Her mind would wander with unanswered questions.

How did he turn out the way he did? Why would he go against his family? Why would he strive to protect any of them? That last question perplexed her, but his support made him noble beyond compare.

Yet, everyone from her family—Starr, Nathan, Phoenix, Declan, Cherry—seemed to hate him despite his recent interventions. And he didn't seem bothered by their response to him.

The exit door clanged open once more and Cherry stepped out with Sally Mae. They'd been chattering away, which died the second they saw her with Carragh.

"See you girls tomorrow," Luna called.

If she didn't take matters into her own hands, Cherry would force Luna into her car, drive her home, and tuck her into bed to ensure she didn't land in someone *else's* bed. Cherry needn't worry. Luna wasn't about to give in to whatever her feelings were around Carragh.

Sally Mae curled her lips between her teeth to try to hide a smile. Cherry sent them both a scolding look but thankfully didn't say anything. Rather, she gave Sally Mae a quick air kiss. "Sayonara, babe."

With hands on her hips, Cherry then turned her sights on Luna. "Luna, love, come over here."

"I'm fine."

Cherry waved her phone. "I got 9-1-1 just ready to call."

Carragh chuckled. "Good woman."

Cherry's face glared at him, but Luna knew her well enough. Cherry appreciated his respect.

"Really. Go home. I'll be right behind you."

"I'll wait."

"No, you won't."

With a roll of her eyes, Cherry threw her phone into her bag and dramatically turned to go to her car.

Luna climbed into the driver's seat of hers and swiveled up to look straight into his eyes. "I can't have a drink with you, and you know why."

"Come with me and tell me why."

His words pulled a laugh from her throat. "That would defeat my protest."

Per his usual, he ignored it anyway. "You asked if I was like my father. I have an answer for you. And to show you how much I am not like him, I won't force you into my car. You can follow me. If you don't, then fine. Your choice." He shut her door and strode away.

The man was teasing her, *luring* her with information. The trouble was, she wanted it—badly.

Cherry's car started up. The queen would likely follow her all the way home. But when she didn't, Luna found herself heading north instead of west, Carragh's license plate in her view for miles as she trailed behind him.

She had questions. He had answers. Maybe it was time for her not to be "the reliable one."

14

On Potee Street, Luna could have gotten on I-895. At East Osten Street, she could have taken a left and gotten on to I-395. Once they were on Charles Street, she could have taken any number of streets to get to a highway. All roads would have eventually gotten her back to her apartment.

Instead, the glow of Carragh's taillights burned her eyes she stared at them so hard. He seemed to drive carefully, slowly, as if he didn't want to lose her.

He turned again and soon they moved deeper downtown, much more deserted this time of night, the tall buildings creating canyons of dark and gray shadows. His car turned onto to a quaint street lined with streetlights that glowed halos in a growing fog.

With a small splash, his tires thunked through a large pothole and then he veered left into an alley. Following him into a dead-end spit of asphalt would be stupid. She *should* head straight home.

He stopped, got out, and gestured for her just as a door cracked open in the brick wall. A couple stepped out into a circle of blue light. A woman sparkling in a dark blue sequin dress took her companion's arm, a man in a suit.

Okay, at least she wasn't about to enter a drug house.

She pulled her car up behind Carragh's. Cut the engine and cracked open the door. So long as the couple were in the alley, she could scream for their help.

Carragh waved to the man who nodded in his direction. Then the couple scooted around the corner. Luna's heartbeat ratcheted up when he strode forward, seemingly impatient at her hesitation.

It had to be, what? Almost midnight? What place would be open now?

His black hair shown almost blue in the dark. He leaned down and placed his forearms on her window ledge. She hadn't even remembered lowering it. That's what this man did to her—blanked her mind and turned her into... someone else.

"This is a little speakeasy that not many people know about," he said. "A friend of mine runs it. You'll be perfectly safe."

"And our cars?" She glanced around. "Doesn't look legal to just leave them here. Or safe."

"Don't worry about it."

She crossed her arms and shook her head. "Carragh..."

He sighed and straightened. "It's legal." He opened her door.

She took his outstretched elbow and let him help her up.

"I'm a little underdressed." She still had on an old pair of Capezio ballroom shoes but just a simple, gold-sparkled top and black pants. The outfit was quite tame for her usual club wear—if indeed that's what this place was.

"You're perfect."

"I'll bet you say that to all the girls you lure to alleys at midnight."

"Only the redheads." He cocked a smile.

Blue light bulbs lined a staircase down into a basement. It swerved right, and she took the last step down—and entered the 1920s.

Red pendulum lights hung over a long bar. Two men stood behind it, one vigorously shaking a martini shaker, another pouring wine. Hushed voices and soft music—not jazz but something more akin to a dance club—floated to her ears. It was nice. Soothing, in a way.

"So, you are a gangster." She couldn't help herself. She bumped his arm with her shoulder.

He laughed. "No, I just like to fly under the radar of prying eyes."

"You like to hide. Or you are hiding me."

"Both. Besides, I rather thought you'd enjoy the privacy."

She did. Her interest in his thoughts grew by the second, but no one needed to know her curiosity got her to follow Carragh into a hidden bar in downtown Baltimore at one a.m. If her sisters knew she'd entered a strange alley and walked down an old staircase to a basement with Carragh MacKenna? Well, every cliché known to the famous redhead temper would be known for six blocks.

Tingles ran up her legs, though, at the thought this hidden place existed in Baltimore. Declan usually knew every place—and often shared his most special spots with Phee. Now, she was the one with a secret.

They took a corner spot and he signaled for her to settle on a long, cheap, black vinyl couch.

"What will you have? Sparkling water with lemon and lime?"

She nodded, a little charmed he'd noticed her drink of choice.

"Coming right up."

After he left her, the details in the room crystallized.

A tray table with a faded gold and rose pattern sat before them. The alcove next to them had two overstuffed, faded chairs in a dusty red velvet with shiny gold and glass tables. Red Cheshire loveseats peppered the room, all placed for intimate gatherings and hushed conversations.

Black checked tiles framed the bar, and framed black and white pictures were affixed to the concrete walls. The light was too dim to make out the signatures scrawled across most of them.

Nothing in the place matched, which only made the space more alluring as if it were cobbled together in secret.

He returned with two tall, frosted glasses of sparkling water. "You didn't get yourself something." The man usually held an alcoholic drink in his hand when she saw him.

"I did. The same as you. I want to talk to you with a clear head."

"About how you're different from your father."

"And more. I'm going to reveal my greatest secret."

Oh. "Why would you do that?"

"To get you to trust me, of course."

The thing was, however, she already trusted him. She didn't trust *herself* with him.

He sat and proved her point. Her thighs warmed from his close proximity. She took a sip of her water. As if it would help her to keep saying "no" to him?

Despite what his family had done to hers, a part of her couldn't help but keep wondering. If they'd met under different circumstances, would she still keep him at arm's length?

Not by a long shot.

15

Luna's eyes held disbelief at his words, but it didn't matter. Carragh had to tell her the truth if they had any hope of moving forward.

She put her pink lips on her glass again. "Your greatest secret? I don't believe in secrets."

That was going to be a problem. He drowned in secrets, though now he wanted away from them. "I'm going to overthrow my father's hold on our family."

It didn't matter if Petra, Sean, or Declan knew about this. None of them thought he could do it. He needed Luna to know—and trust he could.

"What?" She blinked. "How?"

"Being a greater success. Legitimately. The man can't live forever. He's… damaged."

"Like Ruark."

She nailed it—and both men were getting worse. He sucked in a long breath. "So what else can I tell you? You can ask me anything."

She tipped the lime on her glass so it plopped into the water. "Who says I want to know anything?"

"Your eyes. Every time I look into them."

She smiled a little. "And what do you see?"

"Questions. Desires. Ambition."

"Is that all?" She laughed.

He'd inched closer to her so his thigh pressed against hers. She didn't flinch. "I see stars, too. Like in the night sky."

Her lashes fluttered. Ah, he'd taken her off guard.

He was no poet, but the way her eyes sparkled reminded him of the sky over his grandfather's farm—a place he hadn't visited in years since his father sold the getaway as soon as the man was laid in the ground. "The past should be buried, like him," his father had declared.

Carragh sat so close, he could see her throat move in a delicate swallow.

"When you said you killed someone… Was it justified? In defense?"

She got straight to the point. "It was in defense, yes. But justified? Is it ever?"

"So, you do have a conscience."

He chuffed a little, more to dislodge the pain that'd surfaced. It was a small thing, a tiny ache that annoyed more than anything. Damn this woman who made him feel things. "More than you give me credit for."

She thought so little of him, but what had he expected? She'd consider him ready for sainthood?

"You are the architect of your life." She shrugged and leaned over to grab her water once more.

When she tipped forward, a strand of her hair, streaked with gold in the low light, slipped over her shoulder to swipe across her breast. It should have been nothing. Instead, he ached to reach out to finger that red lock, be curiously tender with her, the dead opposite of what he had to share with her. His *life* was dead opposite of her—all rough edges and abrasive threats.

She lifted her blue eyes to him. "You've made choices that most people wouldn't."

"Ah, but you see, I didn't ask to be born into this life."

How many times had he wished it'd been different?

The problem with being a MacKenna had little to do with their illegal past. It had to do with never learning how to trust anyone. Who might want to take him down? Who was working against him? Who might step in and take what they'd worked for? These were all questions drilled into him by his father at every turn.

He was so sick of waiting for a knife in the back, of being a *target*.

Luna, however, didn't want anything from him. And he desperately wanted her to want something from him—not for leverage but for his own future. It was as if only she saw he could be different, he truly could be.

She apprised him. "I didn't ask for my life either—but my sisters and I decided it was going to be different. And we made it happen."

He had her there. It was remarkable, really. In a way, he'd been born with everything and was now trying to pitch it. She was born with so little and seemed to have so much.

Carragh leaned back. "I saw early on how we wouldn't succeed in the long-term on the wrong side of the law. We are better off using the system from the inside."

"You're still gaming the system." She mirrored his movements, sitting back.

The intelligence from this woman was surprising. It was a rude assumption, but there it was. "No games. Just business."

She didn't look convinced.

"I'm going to sell off everything that isn't legitimate. Hell, I'll give it away. But I won't see anything that tests the law in our portfolio. I have other lines of business, *real* businesses

with a future, that we're going to pursue. I'm tired of the…"
He almost said *crimes*.

She blinked at him as if she was waiting for more. That was all he could give her right now.

"I've told you my plans. What are yours?" He really shouldn't be staring at her nipples pressing against that blouse dusted with some glitter or sparkly crap. This woman didn't like to hide—that was for sure.

Her words came out in a flood. "You ask what I want? I'll tell you. I want what I had before your family showed up."

Shot across the bow. Gutsy. He liked it.

She sighed. "I want to dance, grow old with my sisters and their families by my side. I want a house and roots. And I don't want to be in danger."

"And what do you want in a man?"

An eyebrow arched up. "Offering?"

"Yes."

Her thighs tensed a bit as if she needed to squeeze them together tighter. Someone else may not have noticed. He, however, had been studying her body movements for months without even realizing it.

"You can't be serious about me, Carragh. I've seen the women you date."

"Jealous?"

Her jaw tightened, and his ego flared like the easy bastard it was because yes, she was.

"No. Of course not."

Liar. "Well, I wouldn't mind if you were."

"You want to really know what I want? Someone who wants me. *Me.* Not just the girl they think they can't have and what they see onstage. I want a man who finds it easy to be faithful to me. A lover, a partner, and friend. Chemistry and heat. I want it all."

"Tall order."

"Is it? Do you think you should expect less?"

She had a point.

Truth was he could be all that with her, for her. He just didn't know how. But it'd feel damned good to be seen as the man she described. She made him want things, and to have a life that was different than the one he'd grown up in.

"It makes no sense you care what I think about men, you, or anything. Unless you think I'm an easy mark." She shook her head angrily. "Everyone thinks I'm stupid because I dance."

"I would never think that."

"But you have."

She was due some credit for her keen observation on that front. He owed her the truth. "Once. I didn't know you."

"You don't know me now."

"I know enough. How you like the applause but not the catcalls. How you favor your right leg over your left. How you twist those pretty pink lips when you're thinking—which you do a lot, by the way. How when you think something is right, you don't hesitate, like finding your father. Protecting your sisters."

She swallowed. "None of that answers why me."

Why her? She had no idea the impact she could have on a man. How her very presence called up a decency he never thought he could muster. Yet, there it sat on the edge of his conscience—perhaps just waiting for her to finally rise up in him.

He threaded his fingers through hers. "Because you remind me my heart still beats."

His family's specialty was ending things—through protests, power grabs, messing with people's futures. Luna made him want more when they were together. She was the promise of a beginning and not an end.

She looked down at their intertwined hands. "Well. What

do you know? You have a heart." A shy smile crossed her lips, but then she lifted her chin. "So—"

He didn't let her finish her sentence. His lips found hers, and she didn't pull back.

When he finally broke his kiss—and it wasn't brief—all the disbelief he'd seen in her eyes earlier had vanished. Maybe it was the trick of the light or wishful thinking, but he liked it. No, loved it. She might believe him after all.

"Maybe I do have a secret," she whispered.

"Going to tell me?"

"Yes. I was waiting for a reason that I could finally kiss you. Thank you for giving it to me. For being… different from your father."

16

Sean peeled the label off his beer bottle. "You sure this is wise?"

"I need to know who's been talking." Carragh didn't turn his chair around. Instead, he eyeballed the cityscape. A haze had settled, though nothing inside him had. Pink lips—that's all he could think of. Hell, he could still feel how soft and plump they were as he tasted and sucked on them.

Last night wasn't what he'd planned. They'd talked—and then they'd kissed. They talked more. Kissed more. Then he'd followed her home, walked her to her door, and waited in the parking lot until he saw her light go out in her apartment window. He hadn't had an experience with a woman like that —like a normal date—in years. Or was that normal?

He wanted more—and more of that belief in her eyes.

His life was far from normal, like knowing who he could trust. He was about to change that, starting with finding out who was on his side and who wasn't.

Sean scrubbed his hair. "It really could be as simple as Petra—"

"It's not." Such a betrayal wasn't possible.

Carragh spun his chair at hearing his door click open. He rose as Leo stepped inside.

The man had been hovering around his father for years, doing odd jobs, fixing things. If anyone knew what was truly happening, it would be him. He kept his head down, never got arrested, and never disappointed in completing whatever task was before him.

"Carragh. Sean. To what do I owe this summoning?"

Carragh rounded his desk. "Thanks for meeting me." He shook the guy's hand, gestured to his bar cart. "What can I get you?"

"The reason I'm here." Leo slunk to a chair. "You need me to handle somethin'?"

The man got to the point. Good. He would as well. "I need information."

"You couldn't pick up the phone? Traffic outside is a nightmare." He gestured to the window.

"I wanted to look in the person's eyes when I asked it."

Leo slapped his hands on the armrests. "Okay. Shoot."

Carragh settled on the corner of his desk and picked up a paperweight. It was one of the many gifts he couldn't remember getting. Solid clear glass with an Awen symbol floating in its center—three pointed rays shining down from three dots. He rather liked the symbolism of the thing.

"Do you know what this is?" He held it up in his palm.

"Not a fan of riddles."

"Celtic symbol. Related to truth. Understanding it. Loving it. Maintaining it." He set it down. "It's something I reward heavily."

The guy scratched the side of his face. "Yeah, and?"

"I need answers. Let's start with who's been sending messages to Declan Phillips."

"Who's that?"

"Shakedown. Waterfront. Club owner."

He shrugged. "Oh, yeah, the strip joint. Beats me. I wasn't brought in."

Fuck him, he had to keep his ass on the desk and not jump down the guy's throat. "It's not a strip joint. Who's been spreading rumors about me operating against my family? You been talking?" He might as well continue the truth train.

"Talking? What are you askin'?"

Carragh rose, and Sean inched closer.

"Whoa, there." He raised his hands "I don't say nothin' to nobody ever. But there are rumors, alright?"

"Such as?"

"Heard you're not following orders. Going against your old man there. And your penchant for tittie shows…"

Carragh was suddenly inches from the man's face. Sean slapped his chest in the nick of time because he wasn't sure he wouldn't have flattened the man against the sofa until he touched the wall given his assertions about Shakedown.

"A name, Leo."

He chuffed, adjusted his jacket that had gone askew by Carragh's advance. "Names. I got lots of names. A lot of people are talkin'." He leaned forward, placed his elbows on his knees, and regarded the carpeting for a long minute. He then sighed and leaned back. "But there's only one person who never references where she heard it from. Makes me wonder…"

"She."

"Nicole Monroe."

A name he hadn't expected at all. It made no sense that Nicole would put Carragh in the hot seat when she wanted very much in his seat.

A sly smile spread Leo's face. "That one's got designs on you. She makes no mystery out of it, either. Says she could be the one for you—that is, if you'd come to your senses. And women—they make trouble if they don't get what they want. Trust me. I got a wife."

He didn't know that about him. How had he not known? Maybe because he'd had his head down for the last few years trying to put some things in motion. It was like working in a silo of molasses. Circles. Slowdowns. False starts.

And then Luna Belle sashayed into his view, muddling his judgment on top of it all.

"Also, there was that not-so-little meeting of the Monroes and your father last night." Leo eyed him. "I was there. Interesting you weren't."

Carragh hadn't been invited or alerted. So, he was being cut out. Something he wanted—but on his terms, not his father's.

"I overheard Nicole talking to her father in the hallway. Something about a tittie club on the water. Her words." He raised his hand again. "That your Shakedown place? Well, she was saying how it was the first thing she was gettin' rid of the second you and her got married."

"We're not getting married."

He pursed his lips and nodded. "So, you are makin' a move?"

"I've been making my move. But you know that, don't you?" Surest way to test a man? Throw the truth at him, see if he agrees.

"Yeah. Sons. They always want to take their place eventually." Leo inclined his head. "It's gonna get messy. Your father, he likes his…" Leo gestured in the air "…position."

Dethroning anyone—let alone someone like his father— would be. "And you? Where will you fall?"

"The thing is…" he leaned forward again "…what makes you a man is what you choose to do when things are changin' around you. Maybe it's time for things to lighten up a little."

"You saying you prefer my methods?"

"I prefer methods that work. Your father, who I respect very much, by the way, is old school. I won't go against him, but let's just say if things were to change, I wouldn't be unhappy. I'm a little tired of playing the muscle all the time. I got arthritis." He adjusted his jacket. "Besides, the man's not well. I can see it."

"He's fine." Not really, but no one needed to know. The man was approaching 70 and that, between his migraines and refusal to accept times had changed, had to make his blood pressure a mess.

Carragh stepped back to the window. Enough advancing in inches, it was time for him to start making bolder moves. He turned back to Leo. "So, help me change them. Starting with finding out the truth. Is Nicole talking? I want to know."

Leo rose, buttoned his jacket. "Let me ask around."

"Discreetly. This conversation never happened."

"You have my word."

"And Leo," he said before the man exited. "No more spreading rumors around."

He saluted him. "You got it, boss."

As soon as he left, Carragh turned to Sean, who remained standing. "You believe him?"

Sean looked distant. "I don't know. But I got to tell you, Nicole? She could be good to have on your side."

"You like her? Have at it."

He held up his hands. "No, man. I'm just saying…"

"What are you saying?"

"Nothing. Just know Nicole is… and I'm saying this as your cousin, okay? She's a heavyweight in her own right. She would make a good partner."

"I got enough partners." He didn't, but the last person he'd need was a queen bee trying to literally become a queen.

17

Luna pushed open the door of Bloom and Blossom Babies with her butt. Her hands were full of shopping bags, and honestly, if she had more time, she'd have bought more. Who could resist their spring collection?

Little Nicolas would look adorable in the jumpsuit sporting a monkey motif that read "Hanging with Daddy." That boy was going to be an aerialist someday. Every time Rachel brought him to a silks dance class, he reached for the parachute fabric like he wanted to climb.

Then there were clothes for Starr's son or daughter. She got a few things just to get her started—little dresses and a pair of coveralls. The lace christening blanket also was something she *had* to have even if the use of it might not be for a year.

Bright sunshine warmed Luna's face as she paused just outside to hold her face up to the sky. Finally, the sun made an appearance, and for one brief second, everything was right with the world. Her hands were full of shopping bags and her heart was full from being surrounded by little people clothes. No one could be in a bad mood in a baby store.

Then there was last night with Carragh. The man had some kissing skills, just like she knew he would. And he'd talked to her. Told her things. Revealed his secrets. It was thrilling to believe he trusted her with such information, even as vague as it was, despite the fact that knowing such things could be so dangerous.

"You do love this store."

She dropped her chin and her eyes landed on Carragh leaning against his car, his arms full of a flower bouquet. Her heart did a little skip. A quick glance at the driver's seat showed he must have driven himself.

The paper bags rustled against her legs. "Hand delivering flowers to someone?"

"You. It's customary to give flowers to a girl after a date."

"Is that what we had last night?"

"I'd say we had more than that." He thrust the bouquet her way awkwardly. His obvious discomfort amused her. What do you know? Carragh MacKenna might be... nervous?

She didn't need to wonder how he found her. She'd spilled quite a bit last night about Starr's pregnancy and her planned shopping trip. She'd also shared about Phee's teaching and how she hoped one day she had something so big to do as well. Once she got started talking about her dreams, she couldn't stop. She blamed it on his magic kissing.

She set down the shopping bags and took the flowers. Crisp white paper crinkled as she held them close, and a card, buried deep inside, scraped the side of her cheek as she brought the white roses, lilacs, and purple-blue orchids to her face.

"I was going to leave them at your doorstep, but..." He shrugged.

Someone might see. Her sisters no longer lived at their

apartment, but they often stopped by—even still had their keys to get inside.

She read the card aloud. *"You're not the only one who wants it all. C.M."*

She'd reminded Carragh MacKenna he still had a heart—and he wanted it all, just like her. A naive, thrilling hope bloomed in her belly.

He leaned down and retrieved her bags. "Need a lift?" He was being awfully casual for just admitting he wanted more—possibly from her. An intense interest in knowing what "more" looked like to him arose. Overthrowing his father was one thing, but what did he really want? Power? More money?

A chime sounded from her purse. They gazed at each other until the ringing stopped. Once it did, the spell broke.

"That has to be one of my sisters. I'm late as hell meeting them at the dance studio." Phee was hoping to convince them to start teaching in addition to dancing at Shakedown. Like she had time for that?

He lifted her bags. "Get anything good?"

"Clothes for Nicolas and Starr's new baby." She grasped the handles with her one free hand to take them back.

"Ah, starting early. And Nicolas as in Trick and Rachel's son?"

"I'm impressed you know that."

Her phone rang again. She rolled her eyes, set the bags down, and yanked her phone out. "Sorry. I really have to go." Using her shoulder to hold her phone in place, she reached down again for the bags and headed toward her car.

"Miss O'Malley? This is Bly from Sunset Memory Care. I'm so sorry... inform... your father..."

She couldn't catch all the words as the rumble of a car speeding by blocked out half the words. She dropped everything again, plugged one ear, and squeezed the phone tighter to her other. "What was that?"

"Your father," the male voice said. "He passed this morning."

A car horn honked nearby, and she jumped. "What?" Bags rustled near her. Carragh had followed her, and she found herself fitted against him. He was holding her up. "I don't understand," she said.

"Are you alone? Is someone with you?"

"No. I mean, yes."

"Luna," Carragh rumbled near her free ear while the male voice on the other end of the phone kept speaking. She wanted him to stop talking but he wouldn't.

You were the point of contact. I'm sorry for your loss. Come by. Funeral home arrangements. The words buzzed in her mind.

Her phone fell away from her ear. She blinked up at Carragh.

"Luna, what happened?"

"My father." It wasn't time, though. She had more to talk to him about. He wasn't coherent most of the time, but she didn't think when Maven said his passing was close, it would be *today*.

Carragh's arms were around her, leading her up the street.

"But…" she pointed backward "…my car is that way."

He didn't respond or stop pulling her alongside him. Bags rustled. A car door opened. He got her in the front seat. A pressure around her middle as the seat belt was fastened. Her phone. Where was it? Oh, in her hand. She had to call Starr and Luna. She couldn't seem to lift it up in her hand to dial. Or form words to direct Siri to just call them.

The car pulled away and vehicles were all around them. They'd gotten on the highway. She turned her head and took in Carragh's profile.

"Luna." His hand had ahold of hers. "Where do you wanna go? Do you need to go see him?"

"But he's dead." She couldn't see him, right? He was gone. She didn't get to say goodbye. "Sisters," she managed to whisper.

He nodded once and the car sped up.

Her mind was still fuzzy and distant when they pulled into the Phoenix Rising Dance Studio parking lot. The sign—large with a huge Phoenix curled around the P—was the only thing she could seem to see. She got her seatbelt off, found her legs, and was somehow walking toward the entrance.

Inside, Phee and Starr were chatting over something with grid lines. Oh, a schedule. They looked up as she came in.

"What the fuck are you doing here?" Phee's eyes fired toward Carragh.

Carragh. He was behind her. In fact, he had ahold of her elbow.

His voice rumbled. "Luna has something to share with you. She couldn't drive."

"Dad."

Starr waved her hand. "What has he done now?"

"He died."

18

As soon as he pulled into Brown's funeral home, he picked out Luna's car from the others immediately. She needed something new, which he could handle in an afternoon. In fact, he might just call up Tenant's Mercedes and order one from the car.

A beige Buick pulled into the lot behind him, a familiar face behind the wheel.

Cherry unfolded herself from the front and glared at him. The queen marched right up to his window, which he lowered. He'd expected he'd get an angry reception today, but he'd spent three interminable days away from Luna—at her request, so she could sort things. Odd how he'd started to honor her wishes but probably because she started sharing them with him.

"Don't you dare. Not today." Cherry shook her finger at him. He wanted to snap it in two.

Without a word, he got out and headed to the entrance. Let her try to stop him.

"Wait." Cherry stamped her foot. "You cannot charge the building."

Oh, yes, he could. He told himself he came to pay his respects to someone who'd passed. Truth was, not seeing Luna these last few days was eating him alive. Now, she was inside, probably fifty yards from where he stood. He wasn't waiting another second to be with her by standing outside arguing with one overprotective drag queen.

"I know you care about her. So, you will talk to me first, got it?"

Cherry was gutsy. He gave her that.

He gave a tight nod. He didn't take orders, but a little information wouldn't hurt before he went inside anyway.

"Their father died."

The flowers he brought rustled in his hand as he lifted them. "Yes. I'm familiar with why someone would be at a funeral home."

"You would be."

There was an insult in there, but he couldn't care less. He'd been to too many funerals in his life.

Cherry pointed to the door. "They are, too, and shouldn't be."

No question, "they" were the O'Malley triplets.

Cherry glared at him. "All three of them are more fragile than they will ever let on. You don't know what they've been through and—"

"Oh, yes, I do. I know more than you know."

Her brown eyes slanted down at him. Carragh was a tall man. Hardly anyone looked down on him. "Yes. I suppose our Miss Luna has told you some things."

At least she said "our."

The queen continued. "So, you would know they've circled the wagons. You charge in there, you'll force her to choose. And, by the way, you'll lose."

"Didn't think you'd care if I won or lost."

"It'd break her heart if you forced her to choose."

That got him to still. Somewhere between Saturday and today, he cared about her heart as much as his own. And Cherry might be in their court? Shit, he didn't even know he and Luna really had a court.

She lifted her hand. "You want a chance with our miss Luna Belle, you'll listen to me."

"I'm listening." He couldn't believe it, but he was.

"If they see you bulldozing your way in, it reduces your chances greatly. You think Luna, Starr, or Phoenix lived through what they did and would let a man get between them? Don't force an ultimatum between them. You care about her. You wait."

"Been waiting." Why was he talking to this person?

She drew closer. Clearly, she wasn't afraid of him. "But have you tried to get into her world—truly? She's not a part of yours. You want to know how to do right by our little Luna? Understand her world, and I don't mean just catching her shows. Can you roll with that?"

"Yes." He had no idea what Cherry was saying, but if this tall Amazonian was standing between him and Luna, he'd pretty much promise anything.

"Stop trying to lure her into a secret life. Secrets are death to those three. They don't do them—and every time one gets formed, it chips something away inside them."

He understood that, but his life was built on them.

"Right now, she needs someone who will be there. Despite her sisters, she's the most alone of all three of them. So just… be there."

"That's what I'm trying to do." His protective instincts were out of control around this woman. Didn't everyone see that?

"Give them this time without…" she waved her hand "… muddling things in front of everyone."

He scratched his chin. Every instinct told him she was right. He still would claw the walls down to get inside.

He glowered at Cherry, someone who'd known Luna a long time. "For the record, I know what it's like to lose a parent unexpectedly. My mother died when I was fourteen." His throat tightened. "I don't know why I told you that."

A slight smile played on her wide lips. "Oh, honey. Everyone tells me everything eventually."

19

———

Luna's butt was growing numb from the hard wooden bench. The painting that hung behind her father's funeral urn would forever be etched in her brain—every fold in the man's Roman cape, every petal of the bouquet he held out to a half-naked woman. There wasn't anything else to do.

Funny, so many people thought burlesque dancers were risqué. They should check out the paintings that hung in a funeral home. Even the cherubs on two small paintings next to the larger one were barely holding on to the drapes strategically placed across their little pricks.

The entire scenario was stupid. They'd been sitting in this funeral home front parlor that looked straight out of a turn-of-the-century-movie. She half-expected a woman wearing a long gown to come swishing in, trailed by a maid holding a tray of teacups and crumpets, whatever the hell crumpets were.

Maven and Mimi, both former caretakers of their father, had come to pay their respects. The male nurse who had found them, too, delivering the news that their dad had gone "peacefully" and "in his sleep," as if she or her sisters cared.

Then, there was the way Maven kept darting her eyes toward Phoenix. A shudder ran through her at the thought their father had rambled in one of his incoherent gibberings about how he had taken out his drunken rages on their sister. Had he?

More questions piled higher and higher.

Should she have found him again, fourteen years after he dumped them in the care of child protective services? Would Phoenix had been better off not being able to confront him as she got to? Was Starr better off seeing karma had worked its magic on him—taken everything from him, from his body to his mind?

From the time they'd found him until today, she never once asked him her most important question, however. Why did he treat her so differently from her sisters?

The Funeral Director—a Mr. Craddock, Crabtree, Crack-something—appeared for the tenth time, his dark suit reminding everyone of the somber surroundings. "Ladies, may I get you anything?" His face was impassive, his hands folded in front of his crotch as he half bowed toward them.

"A sledgehammer." Phee's tired whisper caused the director's brow to knit but the man backed away, seemingly nonplussed by Phee's reaction. He'd likely seen it all before anyway.

"So, this is how the uncared for go out." Phoenix snorted in derision. "You're put in an urn, placed on a pedestal in a funeral home sitting room, and you wait for no one to show up."

Eventually, the urn would be placed in a columbarium in a cemetery—a little niche in a structure meant for holding such things. Apparently, it was important enough to their father to follow the Catholic guidelines for doing so. He'd left instructions, which was so odd given the man could barely remember their names. He hadn't wanted a full

Catholic funeral with all the pomp and ceremony. Just a simple gathering though he didn't define it.

She was relieved. They could have one afternoon in a funeral home where they normally did showings. And then they could leave the urn behind. She couldn't imagine having the urn in one of their possessions. It was too creepy.

Luna stared at the back of Mimi. "Mimi came."

His former caretaker Mimi knelt on the padded bench, crossed herself, and her lips begin to move silently. It was nice of her to show up today.

Memories flooded in. *Church.* They used to go to church.

Nathan reached for Starr's hand, captured her fingers. She sighed deeply.

Declan drew Phoenix closer. Phee held out her hand and studied her manicure, the Black Onyx lacquer on her fingertips, for the eighth time. "Someone tell me why we're doing this again?" She sighed heavily and let her hand fall to her lap. "I can't believe we're bothering."

"Stop. Please. Just stop." Luna's face grew cold as if all the blood was leaving her.

On the inside, she was brittle and on the edge, and really, Phee needed to stop running commentary on this little… whatever this was. Funeral? Wake? Scene from a movie?

Luna bit the inside of her cheek instead of screaming at the urn that held his ashes in front of them.

Phoenix pulled her top lip through her teeth and then sighed. She put her arm around Luna. "It was nice of Mimi to come." Her bravado finally dropped, which made Luna bristle a little on the inside. Phee truly had changed. Then again, so had Starr, finding a domestic side she didn't think possible.

Mimi rose, announcing she had to go to work. Before leaving, she patted Luna's knee. "It's nice of you three to be here. Most of my patients have no one." No one. That had to be the worst thing in the world.

Before slipping through the door, Mimi nodded at Max, who stood off to the side, hands crossed over his chest, doing that man shuffle dance. Max kept stretching his neck as if his collar was too tight. Which, by the looks of his arms threatening to rip the seams of his jacket, it probably was.

Luna pulled herself free from under Phee's arm and in a rustle of fabric stood. "Let's go. No one else is coming."

Declan removed his arm and rose. "I'll get the cars brought up." Nathan rose as well as if the men were eager to get away from this sad scene and do something.

She understood the feeling.

As they slowly dragged their heels over the thick plush carpeting, the maddening injustice of their life crept up on her in a mad rush. She and her sisters had deserved more.

Perhaps today would have been a good day to tell them the secrets she harbored. The weight of now holding two airplane-sized ones pressed down her body.

First, there was the locket, probably holding one of the last remaining photos of their mother. And the other? They'd never understand her spending time with Carragh. She didn't understand it herself. She just liked him. Felt good around him.

Okay, time to unload one of the secrets she held. "I have something to show you. Something found in Dad's things. I had to pick some up from his halfway house." She reached into her purse and pulled out the folded tissue paper holding the locket that she'd tucked in one of the side pockets. She felt better just having the necklace with her all the time.

By then, Phee had held up her hand and shielded her eyes with the other. "Whatever it is, I don't need to see it."

She held up the locket anyway, and Starr gasped.

Phee finally looked. "That's…"

"Mom's old locket." Starr fingered the silver clamshell.

The chain slipped over her hands as Starr stood and took the necklace with her. Phee and she ogled it, lips parted, eyes wide.

"Open it." Luna stood to join them.

After cracking it open, Phee's eyes misted at the sight. "It's Mom." But then her eyes hardened. "And Dad."

Starr slowly shook her head. "Wow, he looks young."

"She's beautiful."

Their mother's face, framed by her signature long red hair, smiled from the tiny photograph.

The picture curled a little on one side. Starr used her fingernail to loosen the tiny image, which revealed a small picture of the three of them in a pyramid pose with Luna peering over the tops of Starr and Phee's heads.

"Wow, that's a lot of freckles," Starr laughed.

"I'm shocked he had a photo of us at all." A nervous laugh left Phee's throat. "Do you think he ever loved her? Mom, I mean?"

"Not enough. If I could change my maiden name, I would." Starr closed the locket and handed it back to Luna. "Oh, wait. I did."

Phee smiled over at Declan, standing by Max. "I'm going to marry Declan. That's the best way for me, too."

Luna was glad to see as much shock registered on Starr's face as she felt on her own.

"I can attest. Marriage rocks," Starr said.

Phee bumped her with her shoulder. "It looks good on you."

"It feels good." Starr turned to Luna. "You're going to love it, too, L. The best part is when you don't have to worry about other men as much. It's like a guy code or something."

"Thou shall not covet another man's wife?"

"Exactly."

They all had suffered the object-itis that men sometimes adopted. Like they were dolls who had no feelings and were there as their playthings.

"And when you're pregnant?" Starr tapped her belly. "Even strangers get all protective."

"That would be nice," Luna said.

"It'll happen for ya." Starr grinned.

"Promise me you'll accept whoever I choose."

Phee's lips pinched together. "Of course, we would. Why would you ask that?"

Starr's face fell. Carragh had materialized in the tall archway, an enormous bouquet of white calla lilies and gardenias bouncing inside paper that crinkled in his hands. His eyes fixed on Luna. She met his eyes, and just as they threatened to fill with tears, she raised her chin and took a deep breath.

"He probably just came to pay his respects," she said to her sisters.

"He doesn't know the definition." Starr's eyes then suddenly squinched down at her. She was thinking. "When you asked about accepting who you'd choose, did you… Don't tell me."

"There's nothing to tell." Starr's imagination was in overdrive. Everyone was when it came to Carragh—especially her own.

Luna hoofed up to him before Max or Declan got any ideas. "Thank you." She took the flowers from Carragh's outstretched arms.

She faced the disapproving crowd. Declan, Nathan, Starr, Luna, and Max stood in the entryway, glaring at him like he was the devil.

With a huff, she turned back to Carragh.

"My condolences." He peered over her shoulder. "To all three of you." Her two sisters had sidled up behind her.

"Come on Luna. Let's go." Her sisters were behind her, each taking an arm to try to lead her away in a nanosecond.

"In a minute."

The other men continued to pierce Carragh with daggers in their eyes. She used to look at him like that. Now? She wanted nothing more than to disappear into his arms.

She turned to her sisters. "I want to say a little prayer. I'll be fine. I'll see you in the parking lot."

Phee and Starr glanced at one another as if trading a message—one Luna read just fine. "Seriously. He's not going to do anything. You already know Max is going to hover."

He would. He loved to hover—and throw people out of places.

"Okay, but only because Max is going to stay. Aren't you?" Phee scowled at Carragh, who'd grown closer.

Max nodded once and bared a gun inside his jacket. The sight made Luna's eyes well up. "Please." She let all the begging tone she could muster rise in the one word. It didn't help. Max appeared like the granite mountain he always was when he believed a threat was near.

If they only knew Carragh like she did. His family may be a threat, but in her heart of hearts, she knew he was trying to protect them.

Once everyone had left—save Max and Carragh—she went to the altar and laid the flowers Carragh had brought next to the urn.

She then knelt down on the narrow padded bench. She didn't really want to say anything, but she wasn't ready to leave. If she did, she'd be whisked away in a car by one of her overprotective sisters.

The rustle of a familiar suit sounded behind her. Carragh had sat in the front row.

"How are you?" His voice was so gentle she wanted to cry.

"Fine."

"I'm here."

He saw so much in her, it was uncanny. He must see how alone she'd felt over the last few days, not knowing what to say, what to do. A tear leaked down her cheek and she swiped at it angrily.

When had life grown unfair again? Last year—before Ruark MacKenna had appeared—everything was great.

Starr, Phee, and she danced five nights a week. Declan pined for Phee from afar, a constant silent supporter of her sister. Nathan was just the new guy who gaped at Starr with such adoration everyone knew it was only a matter of time before he made his move on her. And Luna had hired a private investigator to find their father—to just learn if he was still alive. There was so much hope all around, so much good yet to come, and they could feel it.

Carragh would have been just a nice guy she met somewhere, then introduced to her sisters, and they'd have accepted him with open arms; at least until they learned about his father. But by then they could have figured something out.

Now, despite Starr and Phoenix's latest happiness, a sliver of anticipation for things to go bad again hung heavy in the air around them. She honestly didn't know what to do next. She didn't even trust her own feelings.

For long minutes she knelt with Carragh at her back, her brain swirling. Without turning around, she knew he stared at her back. It was comforting, as if a hand rested there.

"I find sometimes it helps to just say it," Carragh interrupted her whirling mind.

She sucked in a long breath and let it out. "I didn't find him for me." She blinked at the urn holding what was left of her father's body. She felt stupid talking aloud like this, but her words needed out. "I did it for them. For Starr and Phee to get their final say. And this is going to sound stupid, but

I'm a little insulted I didn't get to ask him the one thing I needed."

"What was that?"

"Why he avoided me during his rages. Mostly, anyway. He went after my sisters more but usually avoided me."

"Maybe he loved you more."

She twisted to meet his ice-blue eyes. "No, he underestimated me. Like I was a kitten in the corner. He assumed I was already weak, cowed." She faced the urn again. "And you know what? I'm sick of feeling like the weakest link."

"I have never seen you as weak."

Then why? Why had their father ignored her? She was sick of questioning that ghost. "Then you're the only one."

"You stood down my father—a man who has reduced grown men to blubbering messes."

"I don't care about your father. Sorry, but there it is." Her knees were growing numb from their position. She pushed herself to standing.

"You shouldn't. He'd been horrible to your family."

She faced him. "But you haven't been."

He slowly shook his head. "But the sins of the father…"

"Shouldn't fall to you."

"They won't soon."

She held out her hand to him. "Then get me out of here?"

20

"Where would you like to go?" Carragh spun his hand on the wheel of his car.

"I wish I knew." Her face had relaxed, and her fingers lay still on her lap.

They'd walked out of the funeral home, hand in hand past Max, the bulldog bodyguard, and through the door. Then again past Declan, her sisters, and Cherry, the overprotective drag queen, to Carragh's car. Their mouths were dropped open, and their protests came in a rush.

She told him under her breath, "Let's just go." She then raised her phone at them. "I'll call you."

"I'll take care of her." He tried to sound reassuring, instead earning glowers from all but Declan. His face remained still as stone.

Luna remained silent the entire drive—except for her damned phone, which pinged like gunfire was going off inside of it. She finally huffed and silenced it.

The highway soon gave way to his familiar tree-lined street. She didn't seem to care where she was, her eyes glazed and staring out the window.

He pulled into his drive and jumped out quickly. Frank, his house man, jogged down the steps to greet them.

"I've got this." Carragh circled to her door, opened it. "Luna, this is Frank. He keeps me organized."

The man nodded once in her direction. "Bags?"

"Hi, and no." She shook her head.

Frank thought she was moving in? Carragh didn't hate the idea, but right now she just needed to be somewhere where she could forget things for a bit.

As soon as she stepped into his kitchen, what she thought reflected in her eyes. Carragh's house was nothing as she'd likely envisioned.

His tastes were eclectic—and all his own. She stepped over to the floor-to-ceiling windows in black steel frames overlooking his backyard blooming with hundreds of daffodils, purple irises, and red and yellow tulips. He rather enjoyed the color.

"Frank, get us some coffee, will you?" he asked the man. "Or perhaps you'd prefer tea, Luna? Sparkling water?"

She smiled over at him. "Water would be great."

"With both lemon and lime," he directed.

Carragh led her down a hallway into his living room. Now that he looked at the room, lined with bookshelves, peppered with art deco statues that stood on pedestals, and modern furniture, he could see her here. They'd spend their weekends listening to music, talking…

"I like that." She pointed to an Erté bronze of a woman holding a peacock feather.

"The 1920s were a special time."

"Full of gangsters." She winked at him.

"You're a little obsessed with gangsters."

"Only one."

A male throat cleared. Frank set a cup of coffee and her sparkling water on a small tray table. "Sir, I'm heading out for the evening. Do you need anything else?"

"No. Thank you." He didn't take his eyes off the woman who just admitted she might be obsessed with him.

He gestured for her to sit on the couch. "You should let your sisters know where you are."

"You'd let me tell them?"

"Of course."

She pulled out her phone and tapped on it, then put her phone face down on the glass coffee table. Probably not wanting to see the barrage of protests coming back in return.

It warmed his chest that she had people who loved her enough to be worried. No one had worried—truly expressed concern—about him in too long.

He moved her silky hair over her shoulder. "How are you?"

"Fine."

Was she? "I lost my mother when I was a teenager."

"Did you get to say goodbye at least?"

An arrow of pain—sharp and hot—ran through him. "No. Do you want to talk about your father?"

"No." But then words spilled from her pretty pink lips. "He wasn't so bad to me. I mean, I got hit but not like them. Do you want to hear something stupid? I broke my arm once. We were playing in a creek nearby and I slipped. When I got the cast, I pretended Dad had caused it. In my mind, I mean. So I was more like my sisters."

He couldn't have unclenched his jaw if he wanted to. "You wanted…"

"No. Not really. But he always went after them first. Especially Phee." Luna rubbed her forehead. "Does that make me sick?"

"No." It made him uncommonly sad. This woman raised

too many emotions in him. "No one should have to endure abuse."

"What was your childhood like?"

How did he answer that? "I was raised to do everything with and for my family. Lots of big family picnics. Then later, dinners out. Every holiday."

"Sounds nice."

"It was when my mother was alive. Then…"

"It became an obligation."

She nailed it.

"Now you want out?" Her blue eyes were filled with questions.

He slowly shook his head. "No. I'm going to redirect it."

"How?"

He'd told her he was going to overthrow the man, sell off assets and more when they visited the speakeasy. Now she wanted more details? He'd give them to her.

"Starting with removing my father as the executor of all the family businesses. Then I'm going to divest myself of them." It should be a relatively straightforward procedure. His father needed to name him, however. None of the other families would leave them alone until Carragh was truly in charge. They'd continue to work around him, with Tomas.

"He'll fight it."

He had to hand it to her. She viewed things clearly. "My father likes to fight. He's kind of lost when things are too good. I think it stems from his greatest fear that he'll be forgotten. That's why he tries to push everyone under him. He'll do anything to retain his standing. And I know just how far he'll go, what he's done." He looked directly at her. "Who he's killed. That's how I'm going to remove him."

Her lips parted. "You're going to turn him in?"

"I'd have to incriminate myself." This woman made him voice truths that even he had trouble thinking of. "But there are things he did when I was young I just can't prove. That's not the evidence I have."

"But it's out there?"

"Someone knows something. I'm going to turn over every stone until I have it. Until then, I'll be sure your family isn't mixed up in any of the fallout. You have my word."

"I believe you."

His shoulders relaxed a bit because it was important to him she did.

"Family is always complicated, isn't it?" She laughed a little, then licked her pretty bottom lip.

"It is. Especially when you let feelings run you."

"You said I remind you that your heart still beats."

"Yes." He could feel it pumping even now. Funny how he'd never thought about that organ before, except when a gun was pointed its way.

She rose and he had no choice but to follow her lead. She placed her hand on his chest right where his heart lay. "Then let's have this night. One single night where… I can feel it against mine."

If it was possible to feel good on this night, she'd found the one loophole that existed to this whole mess to make it happen. As much as he wanted her, though, a tiny sliver of hesitation arose.

"Declan is right, you know. Even if I make things right with my family, you should walk away. I'm no Prince Charming." He could have her—wanted to have her in so many ways. But what do you know? She raised a conscience in him he didn't know existed anymore.

"Who says I wanted a prince?"

"Doesn't every little girl grow up believing the prince will sweep her away after slaying the dragon?"

"Rather, the demons. But that's what you're doing, right?"

He supposed it was true. The problem was his demons

were his own family. But then this woman also had had them in her past—and was finally rid of the biggest one in her father.

Truth? He would slay anything that got between him and her.

She took another step closer so her whole body pressed against his. A low, involuntary growl rumbled in his throat.

Her pink lips were so close… "One night."

He lifted her into his arms.

21

———

Carragh positioned her so her back pressed against the tall poster of the bed. She stood before him, her clothes puddled and abandoned on the thick beige carpeting under her feet while he stood before her the same. He was even larger without those suits, his muscles straining under starched white shirts.

The cuts in the wood ate into her bare flesh. She liked the sensation as it kept her present. This was real. This was happening.

She ran a fingertip along the tattoo on his neck, down his pec dusted with hair as dark as night. His ink wasn't a snake at all, like she expected. Dragon wings spanned across his chest. The creature's tail looped around itself and twisted upward to his neck. She'd been seeing the tip of its red tail peeking from his shirt collars.

When Carragh inhaled, his abs—divots and planes—lifted and made the green and blue scales dance. It was as if the dragon was alive—breathing.

She could see why he had his chest inked, rather than his back. The dragon's pointed head, with its nostrils blowing out smoke, its eyes alight in amber, along with Carragh's face, could then stare directly into opponents he faced. Pity the poor soul who was their target.

The confrontation broke so clearly in her mind. Carragh would shed his shirt entering a fight ring. Lift those large arms so they flexed the dragon's wings. He'd lower his chin as he raised his fists. One look at that tattoo, and then Carragh's ice blue eyes, would burn away the courage inside the fiercest man.

Jesus, her imagination was on fire. Even greater? That ache between her legs had ignited an inferno. She wanted his dragon to burn her alive.

She traced the wings with her fingertip, and his chest shuddered under her touch. Her hand moved lower.

A triangle of softer hair arrowed down to a part of him she never believed she'd get to hold. Her hand curled over his thick cock, and muscles in his jaw twitched under her handling.

Impacting a man—is there any greater power? A little drunk off the idea that this commanding man, this keeper of dragons, who had so many women at his disposal, twitched and growled a little by her small touches.

She swallowed. "I haven't… in a while."

One side of his lips curved upward. "Good."

Tingles cascaded down her legs at the possessiveness that fired in his eyes. He'd give chase if she tried to run now. Part of her wanted to—to feel his arms band around her, capture her body and throw her on the bed.

Wouldn't happen, though. Nothing could make her turn away from this man.

She brought her other hand up to his forehead, moved a curl that had fallen to his eyes.

His hands bracketed her cheeks. Finally, his lips came down on hers. Tongues tangled, lips glided—feasting on her, indeed. He moved his hands to still her hips, which was necessary. Otherwise she'd have slid down that carved bedpost to the floor.

He deepened his kiss and she melted against him as his fingers curled around to her ass. Her feet left the floor and her thighs squeezed around his waist. Granite met her pubic bone as his cock sandwiched between them. Even better, her breasts pushed into the dragon wings, and she swore she could feel them beating.

Air whirled around her as he twisted and laid her on her back against the bed. He caged her against the comforter with his arms, his legs, his torso. He held most of his weight off her, so her hands found the small of his back and she urged him to let go. As his mouth worked over hers, she wanted him to crush her with his body.

She hadn't been much for rougher sex in the past, but Carragh needed to take her, hard and brutally. Make her his, even if just for this night.

Instead, he pulled back. More growls came from him as he lifted one of her legs so her foot rested on his shoulder. His hand circled around her ankle and he pressed a kiss just inside her calf.

"You have no idea the things I've thought about doing with these legs." The vibration of his lips against her flesh travelled all the way to her clit. She had to suck in a big gulp of air and will her back to stay on the bed—not arch into the air like a cat.

He laid kisses down her knee, inner thigh, and settled between her legs.

Oh, God. When his mouth began to work her over, sucking and licking slowly as if taking his time, any control she had over her body flew out into the night.

Before she could come, he climbed up her body and his lips and tongue launched a new assault on hers. More weight came down on her, and his cock dug into her belly. Her hips began to move, seeking him, begging him to just fuck her. She squirmed and bucked against his cock until she was practically riding him on her back.

A low, rumbling chuckle went off in her mouth. His lips left hers. "My little vixen wants something."

"Please," she begged.

One hand covered her breast and his fingers and thumb pinched her nipple. She winced a little, her mouth dropping open into a gasp. He captured her peak and the tip of his tongue swirled around it. His teeth then tugged on her nipple a bit, and little sucks of air moved over her lips.

He moved to her other breast and gave it the same treatment. Her nipples, now hard pebbles, pressed against his chest as he moved back to kissing her mouth.

Pain, pleasure—they really were a fine line, weren't they?

Cold air hit her body as he suddenly rolled off her. He pulled open his nightstand drawer, objects being moved around sounded. He was back, ripping open a condom wrapper with his teeth. It was rolled on him in no time.

He stood, grabbed her legs, and yanked her to the edge. "Need to watch you." His cock found her pussy, and Jesus, she was so wet, his cock glided inside her like they were designed to go together. Maybe they were because she'd never felt this good before.

She tried to raise up on her elbows, but he growled, "Lie back."

She fell back as he forced her legs around his waist. Keeping her eyes on his, he pressed his crotch hard against hers, hitting her right where she needed it. A mewl left her throat and she bit her bottom lip to keep from crying out too much.

He stilled, fully seated inside her. His beautiful blue eyes pierced the growing dark to focus down on her. "I want to be so hard with you."

Even in the dimming light, she could make out muscles in his jaw tensing and releasing as if he had to hold something back. The dragon wings moved along his pecs, as if desperate to be free.

"Yes," she managed to breathe out.

He began to move—maddeningly slowly.

Her hands clutched at the bedspread under her, her fingers unable to get much purchase on the fabric. A sheen of sweat broke out on his forehead. His pace was costing him, too. He didn't need to be so concerned about her. In fact, she was tired of everyone treating her like she was a china doll.

"Carragh," she whispered. "Closer, please." Anything to feel his body on top of hers—he could have anything.

With a sly smile, he reached around her waist and pulled her up to sitting without leaving her. She clutched at him, her hands wrapping around his shoulders, her legs around his waist. He rotated and sat on the bed.

Face to face, she peered into his blue eyes. "I… need." Why weren't more words coming to her?

"Then show me."

She began to arch and tilt her pelvis, moving herself against him. His mouth melded to hers once more and she simply disappeared into him. Skin to skin, they rocked together for long minutes until she moaned loudly into his mouth.

He grasped a handful of her hair and tipped her head back so he could nip at her neck. The delicious pull on her scalp, his arm forcing her against his chest, her insides being filled had her gasping for breath.

He rose once more and whipped her back down to the bed. Finally, he engulfed her with his body, pitching his cock into her so fast she moved higher up on the bed. He then stopped being so careful.

As he thrust hard and deep, faster and faster, the skin on her back burned from the rough fabric under her. It was just the beginning. Soon, she was on fire—everywhere. Any sense of gentleness he might have had with her was gone. He used her body harshly, and she loved him for it.

He was giving over the true Carragh.

A minute later, a cry flew up her throat and out into the room as she shuddered through her orgasm. He followed suit, his growls against the bedspread quieter than hers.

Weight on her body eased as he lifted himself up. He rolled off her, his chest heaving. The room had grown fully dark, and when she rolled her face toward him, reflecting light from the ambient streetlight through the large bedroom window shone in his eyes.

"You are so beautiful," he whispered.

His hand grasped hers, and her eyes stung. Loss. That's what came up in an instant. Already, the thought of being without him took residence in her chest.

He'd made her feel and want things she didn't know existed. Forget what she said about wanting it all. She didn't know what "all" really was—just ideas and concepts that sounded like heaven but had not in any crystallized form in her mind.

But Carragh wanting her as she wanted him? To have her heart, mind, and body filled with him? It was real.

He moved to his side and pulled her to him so her back was against him. Caged, his face in her hair, her chest ached with the reality of their situation.

"Never again. No one else with you ever again," he growled.

Oh, God, why did he have to want her so? "One night—"

"Would never be enough. You and I know this can't end."

She couldn't answer him. Instead, she placed a small kiss on his forearm, his hair tickling her lips. One night was all she'd promised him—and herself. She'd meant it, too. At least when she'd voiced it.

But now she felt his heartbeat against her back, and she wasn't sure she could ever spend a night without it.

"Please." His voice was barely a whisper, and the one word nearly broke her heart in two.

For long minutes they lay there, neither of them speaking due to their strange limbo state—like they floated through space yet were so weighted down at the same time.

How did two people from such different worlds, who no one in those worlds wanted together, end up like this? Clinging to one another in the dark, hoping for things that could never really come to pass.

She must have fallen asleep because sometime in the night, her eyelids drifted open. Moonlight cut into the room. Enough that she could see his blue eyes cast down on her. He'd been watching her sleep.

His hand squeezed hers. Her skin was hot and clammy. He must have been holding it all night as if he didn't want to be separated from some part of her.

She rolled back to face the ceiling, unable to stare into his eyes any longer.

Forget Tomas and his threats, she wouldn't survive this pain that now built in her limbs as if she'd been physically ripped from him.

So, this was what a broken heart felt like.

22

Morning came. She'd woke, cocooned in his arms. She'd slipped free and sneaked out just as the sky was turning purplish gray. She'd jogged down the street and called an Uber.

Once inside, her phone rang. She shouldn't have answered because when she did, his words—"You and I both know this can't end. Please."—every fiber of her being wanted to turn around and go back to him.

It was the "please" at the end of it. The word had pinged around her brain every second since she woke.

Carragh MacKenna was Lucifer incarnate according to her Shakedown family.

He wasn't.

The man she knew was kind, and strong, and very lonely. That last realization hit her heart with such force, she almost directed her Uber driver to turn around.

Instead, she put wheels in motion she knew she'd never get to unspin again. He called. She answered. And when he asked her to come back, she decided. "I'll come to you after the show tonight, okay?" She couldn't leave this man if Tomas put a gun to her head.

"I'll come get you."

"No, please. Let me come to you."

A long silence at the end of the phone. Finally, he spoke. "I'll be here."

It was staggering how happy his words made her. That happiness died as soon as she stepped into her apartment.

Starr stood by the window looking out. Nathan was stirring a spoon in a cup at the kitchen island. Seeing Luna step inside, Nathan put the cup down. "I'll be down in the car."

Starr nodded once. "Thanks. This won't take long."

After Nathan was through the door, her sister scowled at her. "You were with him, weren't you? All night?"

"I'm fine." Better than… She threw her purse on the kitchen counter.

"That's not what I asked. You can't be serious. Carragh MacKenna?"

"You don't know him." Not even the half of it.

"Oh, yes, I do. He's a MacKenna. A family who *kills* people." Starr then raised her hand. "Sorry, but I'm filled with pregnancy hormones that will not be silenced."

Any good feelings she had… vanished. "I'm surprised Phee isn't here for the ambush, too." That's what this was, right?

She huffed. "That's rich. Phee is done with drama…" Her eyes sliced to the side as if caught by a memory. "Which is amazing given how she probably feels right now."

"Oh, and how's that?" Her sister needed to trust her more.

Starr leveled her gaze on her. "Betrayed." She stepped forward. "L. Promise me you won't see him again."

She wanted to tell her everything. How Carragh wasn't who everyone thought. How he'd never let anything happen to her and his plans would make it all better. His secrets, however, were safe with her.

"Tell. Me. You'll. Stop."

"There isn't anything to stop. I just... needed someone and he was there." It wasn't a lie, and there was no time to go into it anyway. Plus, she at least could give Starr some peace, even if such a state might be short-lived. "You both have someone. I have..."

Starr's face softened. "Us. You have us."

"I know." She rubbed her forehead.

"Is that what this is about? You think any of this changes things?" Starr placed her hand on her belly on "this." "You never were the type to just go for someone to have someone."

"I'm not doing that now."

"You know, the last time you got involved with a man not good for you, we lost jobs. But this? We might lose our lives," she said baldly.

"Low blow." Bringing up Rick Kinston, manager at that god-awful coffee shop, from seven years ago? She was young, and stupid, and she'd let herself get manipulated by a boss. Never again. Starr really was all over the place this morning.

"No. It's not. You really have some authority complex, L. Getting involved with a coffee shop manager? That got us all fired. Then finding Dad. Now a MacKenna?"

"Who saved your life, Starr. And Phee's. Remember that."

Starr chewed on her bottom lip. "I sure hope you know what you're doing. Because Nathan and I? We're out. I'll always be your sister. But I'm not putting us through this again. And Phee shouldn't have to, either. I mean, Dad's death—"

"Didn't seem so hard for you. Or Phee." It wasn't until that second she realized how her sister's refusal to acknowledge a huge part of their lives—most of it bad—was just *gone*. "Even if he hadn't been good to us, he was our father. Aren't you sad at all?" Her damned eyes welled. She turned away from Starr.

Her sister's hand fell to her shoulder. "It was hard. Everyone deals with things differently. Phee said her piece. I did, too. And maybe…"

She whirled on Starr and hugged her hard. "I'm sorry."

"You don't have to apologize. It's not your fault for any of this." Her hand cradled the back of Luna's head. Already being a mother. It was uncanny how quickly it happened.

Luna's insides welled up with waves of sadness. Her emotional well had been tapped again and again in the last few weeks—now it was bubbling up all over the place.

"It might have been." Luna sniffed and pulled back so she could see Starr's face.

"Carragh is just manipulating you."

"No. That's not what I meant." She broke her sister's hold and walked to the window. She couldn't face her when she finally bared this next part to her. "The way Dad was with me."

"Horrific?"

She faced her sister again. "No. He wasn't that bad to me. Maybe you don't remember. But you. And Phee…" She couldn't talk anymore. Last night. This morning. It was all just too much.

Starr came forward again, grabbed her by the biceps. "Look at me. If you think Dad's issues had anything to do with you, they didn't."

"Maybe I should have stepped in more." That was it, right? Maybe she'd cowered, gave up, and he knew he'd won. Look at Carragh standing up to *his* father…

Her sister scoffed. "Jesus, L. If this is what being with Carragh does to you… Stop. Just stop. Dad was terrible to all of us. He abandoned us. It was horrible again for a while. We got back together. We made a life. You found him. Phee got to scream at him. I got to as well. Phee is happy. I'm happy. He died. Now, it's your turn to be happy. That's it."

Wow. Starr really had moved on. "I'm not unhappy."

She crossed her arms. "Because of him?"

Luna didn't answer.

Starr cocked her head. "L." Her warning tone, also so mom-like, might work on her future child—but not her.

"Sisters forever. Friends always. I promise." She meant it, too.

Starr just nodded and picked up her purse. "I love you, and we'll get through this. I promise you that. But just… stay away from him, okay?" She didn't press anymore, simply hugged her goodbye.

23

Carragh clicked the lights off except for the Onyx lamp Luna once admired on the front table. He set the book he'd been trying—and failing—to read on marine law back on the shelf. The clock in the hallway clicked its metronome beat, and the quiet drone of cicadas rose behind the glass of his front window. Thirty more minutes and he'd have his fourth night with Luna. It was four more nights than Carragh ever believed possible.

She'd come to him, just as she'd promised, every night after her work at Shakedown.

To make things easier on her, he hadn't gotten within ten miles of the club in the last week—the hardest part of this whole charade. The thought of her on that stage, vulnerable to men's thoughts, her body on display for anyone, raised his most base urges—primarily to stand in front of her, curl her into him and away from anyone else's attention.

He tried not to think about it. It took a supreme effort to do so.

The easiest part of their growing charade was meeting his father every night for dinner, then making sure the car tailing him home got to see him pull into his own driveway. It was an inane game, but it kept suspicions down—or so he thought.

Tonight, Nicole had joined them at the large dining table.

Seated to his right, she'd placed her hand on his father's, blinking her large eyes as if she was Saint Christopher incarnate. "How are you feeling? I've been meaning to drive by more often."

By the way his right eye twitched, her suggestion of Tomas MacKenna having any weakness affronted his ego a bit. "Strong as a horse." He emptied his wine glass and gestured for Mary to refill it.

Carragh barely touched his wine. "You're certainly enjoying your Cabernet." His father normally didn't drink this much.

The man's eyebrow twitched again. "Obviously more than you."

"I thought Carragh enjoyed all things red." Nicole's sly smile made his gut twist in revulsion.

His father lifted his knife, inspected it. "My boy's sworn off red, haven't you?"

"Ask your spies." Carragh threw down his napkin and rose. "Nicole, Father. Papers to sign on your desk, by the way."

They were a benign transfer of assets—something Carragh didn't care how it ended up. It was just one more action to keep his father focused on what he was not doing rather than what he was.

"Leaving so soon?" Nicole sang.

"I have work to do."

"I thought all work and no play made for a dull boy," she pouted.

He hadn't stuck around for any more of her goading. He found once home, however, his mind wouldn't settle on work. Something was afoot between Nicole and his father—and it went beyond a marital union. Too bad Leo had found nothing on her.

The shine of headlights pulling into the driveway crossed the room and interrupted his sour mood. Luna, in her god-awful beat-up car, had turned into his driveway and into his garage. She was early. He'd recognize her dim headlights any day, but they may as well have been a tropical sun by the way they instantly relaxed his chest.

He opened the back door of his kitchen and his arms were soon full of soft skin and her floral perfume. "Anyone follow you?" It was the same question he asked every evening after she'd arrived.

She shook her head. Her forehead was tight, her shoulders ever tighter.

"What happened?" He held her face in his hands.

"It's nothing." She shook her face free. "Starr danced tonight and she kept eyeing me like... I don't know." She dropped her bag on the kitchen table.

"Did she ask anything?"

"No. I just hate how much I'm not telling them."

"So, tell them everything." He didn't give a rip if her sisters knew about their relationship—affair? He didn't know what to call it.

Her eyes blinked and her mouth went slack. "I can't. Not yet."

They went through this every night. The stress of sneaking behind their families' backs hung heavy in the air.

A loud banging sounded on his front door, and Luna shook as if jolted by electricity. Her eyes widened.

Out of habit, he moved to the kitchen drawer just to the right of the refrigerator, reached into the far back, and drew out a Sig he'd stashed here just for these unexpected occasions.

She gasped at the sight.

After tucking it in the back of his pants, he ran his hand down her arm. "Stay here. I'll go see who it is."

"It's midnight."

"I know." Interruptions at this house never meant anything good, but at least they'd knocked. If there were any real danger, no warning would be given.

Sean, arms crossed, stood under his porch light.

He yanked open the door. "A little late for a visit." Sean didn't bother to be asked to be let in, just advanced as if Carragh would move. He didn't. "Well?"

"Your father called. Wanted me to check in on you. Said you were in a pissy mood."

"Don't need a babysitter. Besides, I just came from him. See you tomorrow." He tried to shut the door, but Sean's hand shot out to stop the closure.

"Jesus, man," he said. "Can I least get a drink for my trouble of being the errand boy?" He pushed his way inside.

Carragh let him but only because throwing him out would make the guy wonder what he was hiding inside.

Sean glanced around. "Your father's keeping me busy. He's shorthanded."

There was a dig in there towards Carragh.

"Got something to say to me?" Enough waiting around for the other shoe to drop.

"Not unless you got something to tell me."

Carragh's eyes dropped to the man's hand. It twitched by his side, his stance widened—all the usual tells he was holding something in.

Sean peered down the hallway toward the kitchen, then back to Carragh. He cocked an eyebrow. "So, what do I tell your old man?"

"Tell him if he wants to talk to me, he's got my number."

He ran a finger under his nose. "You burning candles or something?"

Carragh arched an eyebrow.

"Just smells different in here." His lips tightened to a straight line. "Girly."

"It's late, Sean. Talk to you tomorrow."

"I sure hope you know what you're doing." Sean just shook his head at him. "But yeah. Tomorrow." The man then finally strode out the door into the night.

His cousin was up to something. *Fucking great.* He'd have another person to worry about. As if Nicole dropping in tonight wasn't enough. That wasn't coincidence, either.

A creak down the hall—Luna was moving. He strolled down to her before she could emerge. Sean was probably still on the porch. One look at Luna and this little problem of keeping her secret would turn into a crisis.

He slipped inside the kitchen before she could exit. He clicked off the light just in case Sean got any bright ideas to snoop around out back. He walked her backward until she was positioned away from the windows.

"I recognized his voice." Her voice was quiet in the dark.

"You don't have to worry about him."

She ran her thumb across his forehead. "But you are."

Even in the dark, Luna saw so much in him. Maybe too much. "We're going to need to be more careful moving forward."

She nodded, and her arms went around his waist. "Yes." But then her hold released and her hands clasped to her chest. She'd touched the gun, perhaps.

He removed the Sig from its place and set it on the counter. "Don't be afraid."

Even in the dark, her eyes reflecting the lone back porch light shone confidence at him. "I'm not. Not when I'm with you."

His mouth found hers, and she yielded to his kiss so completely, an unexpected relief wafted through his body. Her world didn't include ammunition and watching for cars following her—at least not normally—so he'd expected her to retreat. It would be the wisest course of action.

Then again, he'd abandoned what was good for either of them long ago, hadn't he? But now, for the first time in his life, someone else's life was more important than his own, and he had his lips on her.

24

"Now can you tell me where we're going?" Over an hour ago they'd headed south out of Baltimore and then ended up going east at some point toward the water.

"You'll see." Carragh squeezed her fingers.

He'd said to pack a weekend bag, casual clothes. So, she'd made up a story about needing to go recharge at a spa for the weekend. Amazingly, Starr and Phee had bought it. Of course, she'd let them believe she wasn't seeing him anymore —an Academy Award performance if she did say so herself.

The last three weeks had been glorious, and her sisters would never understand. She didn't even try to make them have to understand. She simply never brought up Carragh, was always where she said she'd be—so she said very little— and the most important thing? She and Carragh were never, ever seen together in public.

Instead, she'd spent long nights in his bed—under him, and on top of him, and any other way she could get. Long nights of being held so close she could barely breathe. She didn't need oxygen. Every day that passed, she needed more of him. She'd have crawled inside him if she could have.

Luna always closed the show with the other dancers, letting Starr dance earlier in the evening so she could turn her pregnant body in to bed early. Phee rarely came to Shakedown anymore. And as for the others? Max, Cherry, Declan, well, they'd learn soon enough she rarely returned to her own empty apartment anymore.

Naps were a must every day to make up for the schedule—getting to him late and leaving early—but it was worth the lack of sleep.

Her precautions hadn't been foolproof, however. After the "Sean incident" as they'd labeled almost being caught, Carragh had rented a car for her to drive, a different one every two days. She still hadn't seen anyone tailing her, but Carragh had been so paranoid about her being seen pulling into his driveway.

His paranoia wasn't completely uncalled for. She'd almost been caught not once but twice by her sisters.

A few days ago, Starr arrived unannounced at her apartment in the morning as she was just getting home from spending the night at Carragh's. Her sister's pregnancy hormones must have been out in full force because she completely bought Luna's excuse about running out for early morning coffee. It'd helped she'd picked some up on the way home.

Phee had been harder to convince, but when she'd caught Luna not at home—at midnight on a Thursday—she'd simply said she'd had to stay at Shakedown for a costume that had to be fixed before the next night.

Her subterfuge options, however, were limited. If her sisters ever found her not where she normally was? Shudder the thought. Cherry already watched her like a hawk, and if it wasn't for Starr's request that Cherry handle her baby shower—even if it was a solid five months away—Cherry might have questioned her more.

She still did, and Luna answered truthfully.

No, she hadn't been inside Carragh's limo in that last few weeks. It wasn't a lie. She'd been driving herself to his place —much to Carragh's dismay, but she'd insisted.

No, she hadn't had any more run-ins with any other MacKennas. That wasn't a lie, either. Carragh had begun having more meetings with his father—at Tomas' place to keep closer to the man he was planning to overthrow.

Carragh shared all his plans with her, and she loved him for it. He didn't keep her in the dark, like so many other men in her life.

Except for this weekend trip that he suggested just yesterday.

She pulled out her lip gloss. "Surely, you've heard enough of me talking about baby clothes."

"You do love to buy them."

"Little Starr or Nathan had to have those onesies." Starr and Nathan's son or daughter would be adorable in them— twenty-six in total, one for each letter of the alphabet and sporting an object to represent them, like an Apple for A.

Carragh just smiled and squeezed her hand. "Ever think about kids?"

"Me? Oh, someday." Or every single damned day since Rachel had Nicolas and Starr's pregnancy announcement. Three weeks ago, she'd have never talked about such things with a man. Now, with every day passing, her biological clock had rung out like a church bell.

His directional signal clicked in the air. "Boy or girl?"

"Both."

"Four or six?"

She laughed. "How about starting with one?"

"Okay."

He couldn't possibly be thinking about kids. Maybe he was humoring her.

"So, where are we exactly?" She glanced around.

"We…" He turned into a dirt drive nearly overtaken by huge bushes on either side. "…are at my house."

"Another one?"

His lips lifted in that way she loved—where a small dimple formed on his right cheek. "I bought it a long time ago. As an escape."

A prick of sadness in her heart went off. Under all that bravado, Carragh carried so much sadness. When he was with her, he seemed happier. At least, she thought he did.

She craned her neck to see what lay beyond the curve in the drive. "My, you do have a lot of secrets."

"Yes."

"And I'm one of them."

He reached for her hand. "Do you mind?"

"Do you mind being one of mine?"

Neither of them answered each other's question. She'd said she didn't believe in secrets. Now she swam in them to protect her sisters from further pain.

The drive turned, and a wide, sandy, grassy area spread out before them, a small white clapboard house facing the water standing in the center of the space.

She pointed to the water. "Is that the Bay?"

"Magothy River."

She'd never heard of that body of water. But then again, she didn't get out of Baltimore much. There was so much of life she had yet to experience when she really thought about it. She and her sisters worked—a lot. Which was probably why they bought her going-to-a-spa excuse. With Starr's belly growing and Phee's aversion to the stage, they all had double the number of dance acts in a night.

Luna deserved this weekend.

She stepped out into a cool breeze. Sunlight sparkled on the dull gray water. "It's so quiet."

"That's why I like it."

They stood looking out over it for a long minute before he grasped her hand and pulled her toward the house. "It's small and basic, but everything works."

She didn't care so long as she got to spend more than one night with Carragh.

The living area was small with mismatched furniture as if things were picked up at a flea market. The kitchen was on the older side with Formica countertops and appliances very similar to what she grew up with.

"You do surprise me, Carragh."

"Expected more medieval antiques?"

"Something like that. How long have you had this place?"

"Long time. I bought it when I was 19. Five years after my mother died. It was completely run-down, but she'd have loved it."

"I bet she would." She circled her arm in his. "I would have liked to meet her."

"I wish you could have." He sucked in a quick breath. "How about some dinner?" He pulled out his cell phone. "I hope you like crabs. Dirty Dick's delivers."

"Sounds great."

While he placed an order for a bushel of crabs, beer for him and sparkling water for her, she moved to the large windows facing the water. A cracked concrete pad held rusted white metal furniture—two chairs and a table. Further down the sandy-grassy back yard, the land's edge seemed to just drop off to the water. A wood pier about twenty feet long jutted out into the water, and a rowboat was secured tightly to its side.

She loved everything about this place. Nothing looked like it would fit with the sophisticated Carragh she knew, yet somehow, it was comforting. Like she wouldn't have to walk on eggshells around fussy antiques so beloved by Declan and Phee.

A loud clang had her turn back to the kitchen. Carragh had rolled up his sleeves and pulled out a large crab pot and placed it on the stove. It was a sight to see. His strong fore-arms dusted with dark hair filling up a huge pot with water. It was oddly domestic and… normal.

She joined him and opened cabinets to find tableware. She fished out a mismatched set of plates. One of them had little blue flowers lining the white plate. She ran a fingertip over the edge.

He winked. "A piece of my mother's old china." He took the plate from her. "It survived quite a few plate-throwing incidents."

"They fought a lot? Your parents?"

"I suppose they did. I remember quite a bit of broken china. My mother wasn't the doormat people believed. She was a lot like you."

"Oh, I don't think people believe I'm a doormat, rather an easy sex doll."

A visible chill broke out on his neck. "Harsh words."

"I can say them now and again."

He pulled her into him. "You shouldn't ever have to think such things, let alone say them aloud."

"Did I shock you?"

"Sadly, no." He brushed hair from her face. "You are nothing like who I expected, Luna Belle O'Malley."

"Neither are you, Carragh." For some reason, she didn't want to say MacKenna. Probably because she didn't feel like he belonged to that name as much anymore in her mind—just like this house didn't seem to belong to the city version of him.

The pot rattled a little as the steam built, so he released her to lift the lid. "Hope you're hungry."

She laughed a little. "Spoken like a true man."

When the crabs did arrive, he began the cooking process while she put the potato salad, coleslaw, and key lime pie he'd ordered in the refrigerator. She then placed the corn muffins in the oven on "Warm."

"If I eat more than one of these I might not fit into my costumes when I get back." She peered at the bundles through the little stove window.

"When you're pregnant, what will you do?"

She swallowed and kept her eyes on the corn muffins. He'd said "when."

His hand fell to her back, so she rose to face him. He stared intently down at her. They stood like that a long minute—and it was then she realized something. She could tell what he was thinking, and he probably could tell what she was as well.

She'd have a family—with him. And he'd do it—with her. And neither of them knew how that was possible.

The pot rattled and threatened to boil over, and he ripped his stare away to attend to the crabs, which was probably a good thing because she wasn't ready to face reality. Not yet.

25

———

"Come on," he cocked his head to the back door. "Let's go down to the dock."

They feasted on crabs and potato salad, and now stuffed, she could use some air. They stepped out into a cool Maryland night, tree frogs chirping, and in the distance, water lapping against the boards of the dock.

He stopped on the concrete pad and dropped himself into one of the chairs. Luna circled behind him. She ran her fingers through his thick hair. She loved his hair. "You look tired."

"Mmm. If I could stay here forever, I think I would."

"Why don't you?"

He captured one of her hands and brought it down to his face so he could press a kiss on her knuckles. "And leave the beauty of Baltimore behind?"

She pulled her hand free, letting the other hand drag down his neck, his shoulder, and bicep. Then she scraped a chair closer and settled into it.

For long minutes they watched tiny whitecaps in the

water appear and disappear. Other than air moving through trees, the occasional bird, some distant boat, the silence was almost overwhelming. There was no quiet in the city—not even in the suburban outskirts. She didn't notice how noisy her life was until that minute.

"It's almost time." He turned his face to her.

"Time for what?" But she already knew, didn't she? She didn't want the dream to end. They'd just gotten here.

"It's going to get ugly." He sighed, leaned forward, and placed his elbows on his knees. He wasn't looking at her. "When we first got together, you said one night."

Her heart nearly crashed to her knees. "Are you now going to say next just one more weekend?"

He turned to look at her. His blue eyes were the saddest she'd ever seen. "I probably should." He shook his head and returned his gaze to the concrete. "But I probably won't. When I asked you about kids—"

"I will." She then flushed as his gaze darted back up to his. "I mean… I want to."

"Would you?" They both knew what he asked. Would she with him?

"Yes. Without a doubt."

"Then you need to know what you're getting into."

"I already know."

"No, you don't, Luna." His lips thinned. "I brought you here because I wanted you to see this house. I knew someday I may have to hide. Or hide someone. I want you to know you can always come here and no one will find you. At least not right away, and then there'd be time to make further arrangements."

"You mean when things get so bad your father might try to kill me?"

"He knows I would kill him if he did that. No, it would be

worse. He would… make you hurt. He would hurt everyone around you."

"You won't let anything happen to me. Or my sisters."

"That's what I'm trying to ensure. But what I'm about to do is going to need to be sudden and the first few days are going to be key. I was wondering if you'd be willing to stay here for a bit. While I handle it."

"You do know I have to go back to work, right?" she laughed a little. "My being here already is an issue. Starr, Phee, and Cherry, they don't really believe I'm at a spa right now. They already suspect. My absence would be noticed."

He nodded slowly. They really had so few options.

"Then promise me you'll come here when I say. Immediately." He rose to standing.

She stood and took his hand. "I promise." Like hell, she'd leave him, but he seemed to need her assurance.

She loved helping him. Being part of something larger than herself.

He circled her shoulders, pulled her into him. "You are important to me." He said into the top of her head.

No man had ever said that to her before.

"You have more faith in me than I probably deserve."

It then dawned on her why her father had peered into her eyes at Child Protective Services that day and not Starr or Phee's.

All he saw when he looked at Phee was the damage he'd caused. And when he looked at Starr, he saw her disappointment in him. But Luna? She'd looked at him like he had the capability in him to fix things. He hadn't, but she'd believed in him back then.

Today? She believed in the man who held her. She was a lot wiser and older now, and she just prayed her trust was well-placed. In the end, however, no matter how things turned out, she'd regret nothing.

"You haven't shown me the whole house yet. Like the bedrooms."

"Bedroom. Only one."

"Good. That's all we need. For now."

26

The next morning when she woke, Carragh was in the shower. So, she snuck outside to call Starr. She'd promised to check in with her sisters, and they'd never know where she was calling from. Besides, she was on a kind of rest and relaxation weekend—something they all sorely needed given the increased dance schedule and recent strains.

Starr yawned a hello. "Are those birds in the background? Where is this place again?"

"Eastern Shore." She was getting too good at "just enough truth."

"Hey, send me a picture of the water!"

She supposed she could. "I will. So, how are you feeling?"

"Dead on my feet. I swear I can't get to the second trimester fast enough." Words she never thought she'd hear Starr utter—ever.

"Well, you're going to love the little T-shirt I'm bringing back for little Emmett or Emma." They'd decided to name their first baby something retro—once again, another thing she'd never thought Starr would go for.

"Don't you dare. I already have more baby clothes than this child could ever wear."

"Okay, but only because you told me not to." Thank God because while she was sure she could find a souvenir shop somewhere, she didn't want to waste any time with Carragh by shopping.

"Good thing you're not here. We had to close. Fire in the dumpster in back." Her voice was so nonchalant it couldn't have been a big deal.

"How?"

"No idea. I swear something is different about this place. But that may just be my pregnancy hormones that are on fire."

"Hey, listen, my appointment is up. Let me call you later?"

"Sure thing. Go. Get pampered."

After she hung up, she snapped a photo of the lapping water and shot it off to Starr, who "hearted" it. Starr and her water…

She headed back inside and found Carragh angrily talking on his phone and pacing, which immediately killed her thoughts of Shakedown and a simple fire that they'd probably put out with a fire extinguisher. Enough people smoked there.

By the looks of things, smoke might come out of Carragh's ears.

He murmured something, then "I don't give a fuck." He killed the call and threw the phone onto the couch.

Damn Sean for questioning where he was. The man knew he had a house on the Eastern Shore, just not the exact address. Something had told him to keep the location close to his vest, even from one of his oldest confidantes. They'd just been arguing too much lately.

Things with the Monroes were taking a bad turn to boot. Shocker.

"Something wrong?" Luna's voice startled him.

"Nothing you need to worry about."

"Carragh MacKenna, don't you start doing that to me."

"Trying not to worry you." He scrubbed his hair. "I've been working on buying more waterfront property."

She gasped.

He held up a hand. "Not for reasons you think. It's so my father can't. But this latest project? Patrick Monroe is bidding for it, too. He shouldn't be."

"Why not?"

"Because he and my father are trying to merge a line of businesses together. No one should be buying anything right now without the other knowing. It was part of the agreement. To keep things on a level playing field. Of course, no one does what they say among the families."

"The what?"

He shook his head and held up his hand. Okay, not in a mood to explain things. She wouldn't be in the dark, however. Not after their conversation yesterday.

"Maybe your father knows about it," she pressed.

"He doesn't."

"So, report it into him. Then offer to bid for it under an assumed name. That way you could own it instead and your dad thinks you've done something for him."

His brows knit in thought as he stared at the wall. "Not a bad idea, actually."

"Your dad doesn't need to know you're doing it for you. Then when you leave, it's in your name."

"A little oversimplified." He faced her and smirked. "But I

like your thinking." He drew her closer. "My little Machiavelli."

She shrugged. "Most men just need a story of sorts—like the men who come to my shows. So long as they think they have a chance with me, they're nicer. Less prone to pushing themselves on me."

"They'd rather win you over than force you?"

"At least most of them. So, just let your dad believe you're doing it for the family."

"I would be. Only my version of family. Not his." She knew about his version.

She lifted her palm in the air. "High five. Teamwork."

He smirked but then ran a fingertip over the shell of her ear. "You have the most delicate ears. They should be wearing diamonds."

"You don't need to get me diamonds."

"Not even one?" He lifted her hand and threaded his fingers in hers.

She swallowed. "Well, someday. Maybe one."

He grasped both sides of her cheeks. "Promise me. No matter what happens, you'll remember this weekend. This house."

"I will remember every time I'm with you—and all the ones to come."

"I'll make sure there are… more, I mean."

"I know you will."

Then, as if to seal the deal, he lifted her up and carried her to bed.

When Carragh gave the signal for her to come to this house, he already knew she wouldn't go. As soon as they got back, he'd arrange for Sean to be the one to drive her. For go she must. Despite her promises, Luna didn't act in her own best interest.

Carragh sucked on the softest part of her neck, just under her ear, as he seated himself more fully inside her. He could drown in her warmth and her undying loyalty to him. The last three weeks may have been the greatest of his life, and he was a greedy son of a bitch. He'd always want more, need more from this woman.

They'd spent all day Saturday sitting by the water, talking. This woman made him do new things—like bare his soul. It felt so fucking great to have someone else know what he was up to—all of it, for he spared no details with her.

She came up with ideas herself. This woman was no dummy.

Buy a small property completely away from the waterfront and gift it to his father. In other words, misdirect the man's interests.

Ask to come to Sunday dinner before he asks. In other words, lead him on.

Tell everyone around him about his father's latest win, though she had no clue what that meant. It could so easily mean another person's death—but it'd feed his ego.

This woman knew men—and he was going to be sure from this moment forward he was the only one in her life of consequence.

She let out a moan. She was close—and he was going to draw it out. He pulled out, earning a mewl of protest from her throat.

Red tinged her chest, and her soft skin flushed as he crawled down her body. He grasped handfuls of her thighs while she grabbed fistfuls of his hair. He then dove straight for her sweet pussy.

She would be his every night if he could. But the only way he could have this woman was for his plans to go forward, no mistakes. Timing was going to be everything. And then? He had plans for Luna Belle O'Malley—so many more nights of her squirming under his hand, his mouth, his whole body, whispering his name in the dark.

Wet coated his mouth as she came hard, and he held her legs open. When her shudders calmed, he climbed back up to take her mouth and thrust back inside. She was more than game as her leg hooked over his and her hands pressed his ass down. She wanted more. His little vixen was a sensual thing, which was good because he was only getting started on her tonight.

"Carragh," she breathed. "Fuck me."

Permission granted, he took full advantage. His hips pitched into her, driving himself even further until she was making those sharp cries she made when she was close to another orgasm.

He fucked her furiously, staring down at her beautiful lips twitching and open in pleasure. He fell to her and their mouths melded once more. Teeth and tongue grazing, her chin must have been raw from his rough beard.

Her fingers threaded in his hair as she tightened around his cock. He let go and pinned her to the mattress with more weight so he could grind out her release.

An involuntary grunt came from his throat as he came a minute later.

His sweat-soaked chest glided over her breasts as he flopped over to his side, his hand roughly capturing her arm as he breathed up to the ceiling. "Fuck *me*."

Her head fell to the side, and his gaze met hers. "I think you just did."

A hearty laugh built in him until the bed shook under

their joined laughter. But it died sharply as if they both real-ized this weekend was a temporary respite.

Their situation was no fairytale. He peered into her trusting eyes, half in love with her, and vowed to do every-thing to keep it from growing into a nightmare any more than it was.

27

As soon as Luna stepped through the makeup door, Cherry rose to her full height and crossed her arms. "How was the Eastern Shore?"

"Relaxing, where is everyone?" The usual rustle of costumes being put on and the scent of wax and eyelash glue was conspicuously absent.

"Starr has morning sickness, Nikki has the flu, and Sally Mae and Cortelana are on their way, so you have exactly fifteen minutes to spill it, girl." She waggled her index finger in air circles.

"What are you talking about?" She threw her bag near her stool and a waft of dust rose up.

"Spa, my fine black behind. You know you can't hide your sneaking around from me any longer. Starr shared the picture with me—a picture that was taken not a hundred miles anywhere near a spa. I've got eyes."

Now her heart sank to the floor. "Does Starr suspect?" She didn't want to worry her.

"Oh, I'm sure both of your sisters suspect something's up,

but they wouldn't ever in a million years dream you would actually go away with that man."

Luna knew this day would come, when everyone around her had had enough of her choices. Well, she wasn't having any of it. "Everyone needs to understand I'm a grown woman."

"Who is being lured—"

"No one's *luring* me. I might be in love with him." She'd had it with not voicing her real feelings.

A cane rap on the door frame sounded. "Ladies."

Cherry straightened the little pots of concealer and other makeup on her stand. "Declan, she is all yours." She waved her manicured hand in the air. "Maybe you can talk to some sense into our little Miss here."

"Luna, can we talk in my office?"

Here came the lecture. She was really getting sick of being handled. She marched around Declan and straight to his office.

As soon as he closed the door behind her, she spoke. "It's not what you think." She wasn't waiting for him to start the "watch yourself" talk.

A puff of amused air left his chest. "And what do I think?" He limped to his desk leaning on his cane, moved a huge bouquet of daffodils and daisies over, and sat on the corner like a disapproving principal or something.

"I'm sure nothing good." She raised her hands in the air but then dropped them to her sides. "But please, remember, Carragh intervened with Ruark when he attacked Starr. He did it again when Ruark came back for you and Phee." It hurt to say the words, but they were necessary.

"No one should ever have been in the crosshairs of anyone to begin with."

"He's on our side."

"I seriously doubt that."

"Why? Why such doubt when he's shown nothing but goodwill to all of us?" Luna stepped forward. "In fact…" Her words died. She'd almost given up his secret. She shouldn't. "You can trust him," Luna said harshly. She fingered one of the daffodils in the vase.

"They're from Cherry's garden," he said and stood. He rounded his desk and dropped himself to his chair. "She found out daffodils were my mother's favorite."

She looked over at Declan. "They were Carragh's mother's, too."

He took in a long breath. "I know."

"Did you know her?" She really wished she could have met her.

"No, but she and my mother had been friends when they were young. I knew that from reading her diaries."

"Oh." A vein of courage burst open. She was going to have to take a chance, that Declan was who she believed him to be —wise, a true friend, and believed she was an *adult*. "He's going to overthrow his father's hold on things. He's trying to make things right."

"I know that, too." He set his cane against his desk. "But he's about to engage a war, Luna. Do you realize that?"

"He said as much. But he won't let anything happen to me."

"If you think he can protect you, you're wrong. He may want to, but that doesn't mean he can."

"I know you're worried."

He leaned back in his chair and steepled his hands. "Worry isn't the half of it."

"The truth is, Declan, I can't stay away from him. I…" Why couldn't she just say it? Would it make any difference in how Declan felt? *No.* But if she voiced it, somehow her love for him would sound cheap, like she was a whiny little romantic who wasn't thinking straight. On the contrary, she felt she was thinking straight for the very first time.

Declan sighed. "You were right when you said you're a grown woman. But know this. If it comes down to his life or yours—"

"He's made arrangements." At least that's what she'd call his safe house. She shuddered to even think she'd labeled it in her mind already.

"What kind of arrangements?"

"Just trust me, Declan."

"You're sounding more and more like Carragh every day, Luna. It worries me."

"Maybe this is who I was all along." She was beginning to feel more… stable and grounded. Or something. "I really wish people would stop treating me like I'm infatuated and seeing things through rose-colored glasses. I would never do anything to put anyone else in danger. Contrary to what everyone around me seems to think."

"No, I know you're smarter than people give you credit for. But now, I'm going to tell you one of *my* secrets. I'm going to trust you will keep it under your hat. That's how much I trust you. *You*, not Carragh."

"I'm listening."

"Tomas has been laying low with us for one reason and one reason only. I have his sister's diaries. They are… incriminating."

"They would be considered hearsay and not admissible in a court of law."

He half-smiled. "I knew you were smart. But they can be rather helpful in shaking out people who have wanted to talk for years. People Tomas has not been so… good toward. I have dozens of her Moleskine books. Pages of entries in her hand. She didn't miss a day for years." His eyes bore down on her. "She recorded a lot of her family's comings and goings—and things she overheard, especially about Tomas."

"Carragh is nothing like his father."

"That may be, but his father is a killer. I have half a dozen entries that describe, in detail, things he executed himself."

On the word "executed," a shudder ran through her.

"That is the right reaction," Declan said.

"Why didn't you ever leave Baltimore if they were so bad?"

"Because it wouldn't have mattered. They'd have found me anyway. A life on the run is no life at all. Here, I have friends, a life."

She stood. "Then you understand why I won't leave or be told who I can and cannot love."

His face shifted. She'd surprised him. "Are you sure you're in love with him?"

She hadn't been until that very second. "Completely."

28

———————

The Owl Bar was quiet for a Tuesday afternoon. With two fingers, he tipped his glass back and forth on the cocktail napkin. He'd needed a drink after his last little showdown with his father earlier in the day.

His father's words rang in his ears.

This little dalliance of yours has gone on long enough.

Burn it down. Burn Shakedown to the ground.

I'm sick of this thorn in my side.

End your childish obsession.

Carragh had stormed out without as much as a glance back. Guess that was the end of the family dinners.

He glanced at his watch. Sean was late.

Tonight, Carragh finally folded his cousin into his plans—and starting tomorrow, the final pieces would be put into place before any more of his father's plans were enacted.

The door opened behind him and a familiar female voice tittered, "No, I'm fine. There he is."

As if today couldn't get any worse… Nicole clicked up to him wearing that senseless fur coat and yet another too-tight dress. She stopped in front of his table.

"Heard you wanted to talk to me."

"Where'd you hear that?" His breath fogged the glass.

"Around. I hear a great many things." She delicately dropped into the bench seat next to him, her fur coat dripping off one shoulder. "Okay, it was Sean."

She'd likely made that bit up. "Thought fur was out of fashion. Cruel, actually."

She shrugged, reached over, curled her hands over his, and took his glass.

"You do like taking my drinks from me."

"Not in a sharing mood?"

"No."

"Neither am I." She scooted a little closer and placed her hand on his leg, which chilled him to the bone.

He swung his gaze to her, which earned a smile. Her lipstick bled around on the corners of her mouth.

"I'm here to tell you that I want you to go ahead." Her breath stank of liquor.

"Go ahead what?"

"Go ahead and fuck her all you want. Get her out of your system. I don't mind." She nearly sang the words as she lazily lifted the glass to her lips and took a sip. "Mmm, you have good taste in drinks, at least."

Nicole had been taking a page out of his father's book. So predictable.

"You been planting rumors about me." He made it a statement just to see if she'd have the gall to deny it.

The more he thought about the swirling rumors, the more it made sense the chatter came from her—and mostly her. Leo still hadn't raised up any evidence that *didn't* lead back to Nicole Monroe. "Talking to my father... and others."

"We're concerned about you, that's all." She actually sounded sincere—the only shocking thing to come out of her mouth since she'd slithered her way into his space.

He turned to her. "Stop."

Her lashes blinked slowly. "No." She eased out of the booth but leaned down to give him a shot of her ample cleavage. "*I'm* the best lay you'll ever have."

Maybe he'd had it wrong all along. His father wouldn't be the most difficult obstacle in his family turn-around plans. One brunette with a delusional queen complex might be.

"Good night, Nicole."

She smirked, straightened, and without a backward glance, headed out.

He was going to do the same—once he gave her a head start. Five minutes later, he left a hundred under his empty glass, and once through the door, headed up the street. He needed to walk. Think. He put his phone on silent. He'd find out where the hell Sean had gone later.

Six blocks later, Carragh got real with himself. He was out of time. It was only a matter of time before Luna ended up dead—all because his heart demanded a starring role, leaving his brain back home in a closet somewhere.

His father's motives were often as clear as dirt, but not his plans for him. The man had figured out Luna was important to him. So now? He wanted Carragh broken—crippled and unable to take his rightful place as head of the family. Her demise would be an accident, of course—car accident, mugging, asphyxiation from a gas stove left on. It could be any one of those so long as his father had his way.

Or the man wanted him worse than shattered, for that's what Luna's death would be to him. The man wanted him so angry and revenge-thirsty he'd fall into his father's line of work with gusto.

Jesus, his mind was playing tricks on him. His body, however, got himself to his car, and within forty minutes he was pulling into Shakedown's parking lot.

By some divine signal, he thought to glance at his silent

phone. Sean's number lit up his screen. "Where the fuck were you?" He had no patience for pleasantries.

"Where the fuck are *you*? I'm at Baltimore Memorial. Your father just had a stroke."

29

Hospitals. Fucking noisy places. Beeps, squeaks on sheet vinyl floors, doors opening and clicking shut…

Carragh stared down at his father. Even engulfed in half a dozen stiff white sheets in a bed with plastic girders, the man spilled out in all directions. He was pale. His face shrank on one side.

He barely heard the doctor. "He's been stabilized. We're waiting on a few more tests before we do a CT scan…"

His father murmured something unintelligible.

"It may take a bit for him to regain his language skills."

Language skills? Is that what they were calling it now? "Thank you, Dr. Madris. Give us a minute, will you?"

"Of course."

His father lay still except for his chest rising and falling. It was an odd thing to see one's father so idle and feeble. As much headbutting as they'd done, a strange discomfort had taken ahold of him at seeing the man so impotent. He wasn't sure how to feel about it.

Sean sidled up to him.

"Where was he?" Carragh asked.

"His office."

Of course, he was. It was where he spent most of his life. "Who found him? You?"

"No, Mary. Called an ambulance. She tried to get ahold of you. Repeatedly."

He swung his gaze to the man. "Are you seriously giving me attitude now?"

"You were with her, weren't you?"

"Hallway."

The hallway was empty, but he lowered his voice anyway. "None of your damn business."

"I would say it is my business now. Your father is in the middle of his first business transaction with the Monroes, and you should have been there—"

"We're pausing the deal."

Sean's lips parted. "Tomas would want it to continue."

He slanted his eyes down at Sean. He'd never seen the man dig in his heels so hard. "What the hell would you know?"

"I've been in every meeting. Have you?"

He hadn't. "We're waiting, Sean." The ability to delay things a bit was a blessing in disguise. "No arguments."

Carragh waited to see if his protests—which he could see as clear as day sitting on his lips—might come out. They didn't.

"I'm getting some coffee," he finally said.

"Go home, Sean. I've got this."

He nodded once and didn't look happy, but really, who cared right now?

Now to secure a certain redhead. He dialed Luna's number and was forced to leave a message. She was probably onstage, being eyed by other males. Fuck him. He had a lot to do—and all of it needed to be done at once. Jealously would have to wait another day.

He had needed a window of opportunity to make his move, and by some damned miracle, he was getting it.

Luna should be dead on her feet. She'd done three solo acts, two duets, and now the final night's ensemble. The Steamboat Sally routine didn't seem to have its usual effects tonight on the crowd. Maybe they were as bored as she was. Then again, maybe she just had better things to do—like focus her attentions on a certain man.

She felt uncommonly good. *Guess this is what being in love was like.*

She slammed her trunk shut after securing her two bags. Her costumes needed serious cleaning—especially her blue velvet dress.

The glow of a cigarette in her periphery caught her eye. It was late, and just a few cars peppered the lot. Starr and the other dancers were long-gone.

A few cars over, a brunette in a black coat leaned against a car, staring hard at her. She pitched the cigarette, still lit, to the pavement and pushed off. There was no mistaking she was headed Luna's way, and as she grew closer, Luna recognized her as Nicole Monroe, the woman Carragh was supposedly not engaged to after all.

"He's never going to marry you, you know."

Here it comes. The jealous woman tirade. Luna had been embroiled in many over the years, all of which proved stupid given she'd never steal another woman's man. It usually started when a man just looked at her onstage.

"Who? And who said I wanted to get married?" *Playing dumb seemed the wisest course.*

Nicole swayed a little on her feet. "Oh, you're going to act stupid." She reached into her bag and brought out another cigarette. "Well, you do strip for a living."

Luna's spine wanted to snap in two. "I dance. Big difference. You need me to call you a cab?"

Nicole snorted and lit her cigarette. "A cab? You have got to be kidding me." She drew closer, blew smoke in her face. The cigarette twiddled between her two fingers.

Luna kept one eye on it and one eye on Nicole. That was the thing about growing up with a drunken father who smoked. You learned fast to dodge the sparks—or the burning end of it. "It's late, Nicole. Go home."

She smirked. "You know my name. Very good. Then you know Carragh and I are engaged."

"No, you're not." She should not be arguing with a drunk, green-eyed woman, but she was going to stand up for herself —and her future.

Muscles in the woman's jaw twitched and she and her lit cigarette breached the final inches of polite space. "If you care about him, you'll stay away."

The clatter of the exit door sounded behind her. Declan filled the doorway.

"Luna." Declan's voice carried across the parking lot.

"Be right there." She turned back to Nicole. "Good night, Nicole."

Nicole grasped her arm—hard—and cigarette ashes and sparks fell to her skin. "Remember what I said."

Luna yanked her arm free and brushed the ashes off her skin, which left a smudge. She spun on her heel and headed toward the club. There was no use in arguing with the bitchy woman.

"Who is that?" Declan raised an eyebrow.

"No one." She glanced back to see Nicole getting in her car. "I was just heading out. Need something?"

"That one of Carragh's girls?"

Luna shrugged.

"I don't suppose there is anything I can say that would make you stop."

He didn't pose it as a question. They both knew the answer anyway.

"No, I see not." He sighed heavily. "Come on, I'll get you to your car."

Her car was only fifty feet away, but she let him play the overprotective, maybe-soon-brother-in-law. An odd thought entered her mind. If he did marry Phee, he would be her family, which oddly would make her then distantly related to the MacKennas given Declan's mother was Tomas' sister. Talk about a tangled family web…

She drove straight home and was cognizant enough to watch to see if drunk Nicole might be tailing her. No one seemed to care who she was—she just encountered the few anonymous drivers of a late Baltimore evening.

When she pulled into her parking lot, Carragh's car idled in a spot near the one she always took. He'd left her a message earlier, saying he missed her. They'd planned—on purpose—not to see one another tonight. To say she was thrilled he showed up was an understatement.

But then he stepped out of his car, his face a mask of shock.

"What's wrong?" she folded herself into his chest.

"I just need you."

"Then stay with me tonight." They never stayed at her place, but it was high time they got to go wherever they damned well felt like it. There was no need to bring up Nicole's visit. The lines around his eyes were already deep enough for one night.

Once inside, he simply pulled her to the couch and started talking. She learned about his father's stroke and so many details about the moves he needed to make tomorrow she couldn't keep them straight. But it dawned on her when the clock struck 4 a.m., she trusted Carragh more than any man she'd ever trusted in her life. In fact, she may have never fully trusted a man before him—not even Declan.

30

"A shame to hear about your father." Patrick Monroe at least sounded sincere. He shook the ice in his glass. "So… you taking over now?"

"My father will be fine, and yes." Carragh twisted his glass of vodka, not having touched a drop. "But I'd like to take a look at our agreement letters again. Make sure I won't…" How to phrase this?

"Fuck anything up?" Patrick Monroe finished.

"Hmmm." It'd been a busy few days. His father had been transferred home with strict orders to rest. Carragh, however, couldn't afford a single moment of downtime. He had to start with unraveling anything his father had started.

The man stood, straightened his jacket. "Out of respect for your father, I'll slow down. One week. Then we'll need to make other arrangements."

Time—there was never enough of it. "Just business, right?"

"Always."

They shook hands, stiff and just barely cordial. Patrick didn't trust him. Well, he didn't trust the man, either.

As soon as Patrick left his father's study, Sean rose from his lurking position in the corner. "You sure this slowdown is wise?"

"Yes."

He scrubbed his hair. "He's not going to wait forever, and your father would—"

"Would what, Sean? You seem to have an awful lot of opinions on my choices."

"It's just I don't want to see things go south, that's all. You've been a little distracted lately."

He had been, but not for reasons Sean could guess.

Carragh just shook his head and stepped through the set of glass French doors.

"I sure hope she's worth it," Sean mumbled.

He pivoted. "What did you say?"

"Not like you to overthrow everything over a girl. You—"

"I what?"

"Family first, that's all I'm saying." He held up his hands in surrender.

"Exactly what I'm doing. Taking my rightful place as head of this family." He got six inches from the guy's face. "And if you've got a problem with it, state it now. *Cousin*."

"Jesus, no need to wave your testicles around." He backed up, dropped his head a little. "I got you, okay?"

"You better have."

"I do, man. I do."

They stood there for a long minute until one side of Sean's face tugged up. "So, let's go out. Celebrate. Drinks on me." He slapped his shoulder.

"It's late, Sean. See you tomorrow." A drink was the last thing he needed. What he needed was a certain redhead.

31

———

Luna grinned wide at the adorable couple nearest the stage. She was a petite brunette who had her arm looped through his. They smiled up at her but kept glancing back at one another. So much love passed between them her heart thumped inside her ribs.

If she'd met Carragh under different circumstances, that could be them.

A tickle arose in her throat a little as she pranced across the stage in long, confident strides, her leg peeping through her gown's long slit. What was up with their filtration system? The air smelled strange.

She raised her arms wide along with Nikki, who was gesturing wildly for more applause. They'd teamed up for this new routine—a cute little number where they tried to outdo one another in their ode to Marilyn Monroe. Nikki chose to wear the famous white halter dress and have it blow up around her ears. Luna donned a pink satin gown similar to the one Marilyn wore in "Diamonds Are a Girl's Best Friend."

People were rising and moving, their faces darting

around. Loud shouts in the back could be heard over the trumpet blares of the music. That's when she realized something in the club was wrong.

There's a saying that gets drilled into every performer: the show must go on, no matter what. You didn't skip rehearsals—ever. You didn't leave the stage unless you broke something serious, and even then, you'd stay on and smile.

Stage lights warmed the air, some nights to the point she danced through what felt like a heatwave, but tonight they were too hot. Maybe the filters needed changing? Her body rocked, and her head swam, but she had to keep going.

The crowd just needed a little more incentive to keep their eyes where they should be—on the stage. She turned and sent her fingers to the zipper of her long pink gown. Glass breaking sounded behind her. There went more of Declan's beloved stemware. She coughed a little as an acrid smell invaded her nose.

A loud, piercing alarm assaulted her ears, and someone screamed behind her. She pivoted quickly. The cigar smoke had changed to something sharper, more like acid, burning her throat. Her arm lifted to gesture to the crowd and her hand parted smoke, twisting and turning in front of her.

Her shoe slipped on the stage, and her hand reached out to grasp the red curtain behind her. A loud rip rounded, and at the top, a gray mist blew through the hole.

More cries and shouts came from the dark, and the loud piercing got louder. It nearly split her eardrums. Before she could register what was going on, someone cried "fire." A bright orange glow shot up from the back, like angry arms rising to the sky. And then the flames were everywhere. They climbed the walls so fast, almost like liquid.

Her hand flew to her throat, and her vision grew hazy. *Wet.* A mist was falling from the ceiling—all over the patrons who were pushing and shoving their way to the back. They ducked their heads like they'd stepped outside into the rain.

The garage doors flew up on the side. Someone had opened it, and the smoke streamed for the exit. *Poison.* The air tasted like poison.

God, she was so dizzy. The floor began to tilt, and she fell to the warm floorboards of the stage.

Nikki jetted past her, but she couldn't move. She couldn't see; the room had filled up with dark, gray clouds. Then everything was alive with flames—the dining tables, chairs, walls.

She pulled in a reedy breath and little dots formed in her eyes. The curtain fringe curled up and turned black. Someone was pulling on her. Dragging her legs.

Crackles and hissing and shouts began to fade as she stumbled into the concrete hallway. People were heading out the exit door. She lost someone's hand. Cherry's?

Men were shouting just outside the door.

A huge roll of smoke overtook the hallway, and the floor rose up and caught her as she slid down the side of the wall, the gravelly surface cutting her cheek.

As Carragh took the highway exit, the sunset came into view. The sky was a beautiful bright orange. In fact, it looked alive. Look at him, noticing sunsets.

He'd had enough hiding. He was collecting Luna, taking her to his bed, and he didn't give a fuck who saw it all happen.

His car stopped at a stoplight, and the sounds of sirens and the honks of fire trucks filled the air. So typically Baltimore. He peered out the windshield. Man, the sky was incredible. The light changed, and he rounded the corner.

Blue flashing lights of a cop car spun in front of him so fast, he had to nail his brakes.

He turned yet another corner and his brain froze. It couldn't be.

His body lurched forward as he slammed his car into park, angled in the street. Abandoning it, his feet pounded the pavement. But then the sound was lost by the rumbles of firetruck engines and the roar from the flames. Shakedown was engulfed in pure hellfire.

Red and blue lights flashed through the air as the firemen held firehoses aimed at the roof. A few others were shouting at people to stay back.

Jesus, the fire was so loud.

Figures silhouetted in an orange glow huddled together between the trucks and cars. Some were walking aimlessly about. Some gaped at the building being consumed. Other's faces were streamed with tears, the wet reflecting firelight.

Shouts and loud hacking at the back door on the side of the building unstuck his legs. He moved closer until he hit a wall. The heat—God, the heat from even 100 feet away was an invisible barrier he couldn't seem to push through. His lungs constricted from the smoke that hung in the air like thick curtains.

A loud crack and glass burst onto the front walk; the front door had nearly exploded from the heat and pressure. The front of the building was nearly unrecognizable. The awning, long engulfed by fire, was nothing but wire sticks that sagged to the side.

Luna. He scanned the crowd, which was futile. She wasn't yet out of the building. He didn't know how he knew it. Call it a sixth sense. Call it some primal tether she had on him. But she was inside.

Fury threatened to choke his throat. "Luna?" he shouted into the blaze. His shout was lost in the roar.

Fuck the hell raining down on the earth right now. It could scorch his skin off his body, melt his bones, but he was going inside. She might be alone, scared witless.

With his mouth and nose in his elbow, he advanced anyway into the overwhelming putrid smoke and firestorm. Muffled shouts rang all around him. The skin on his face scorched and his eyebrows seemed on fire. His legs still moved—at least until arms banded around him, dragging him backward.

He shouted her name again and again while he bucked out of the hold and landed a hard blow on whoever dared to keep him from going in.

A loud crash brought down the back part of the roof, and a bellow of ash and smoke rose to the sky.

No time left. Fuck this demon raging in front of him. He made a laser dash to the exit door, a giant crease down the middle like it'd buckled in the heat.

More firemen; huge yellow-clad arms were around him again, yanking him back. A rough voice screamed in his ear, "Get back."

Like hell. They'd have to shoot him to stop him. They still managed to yank him back a few feet. The exit door clanged to the side, and through a huge cloud of smoke, Luna's red hair dripped over a fireman's arm. Then Declan was being dragged between two others.

He stumbled forward, put his hand on her head, and came away with blood. He followed them to the open door of an EMT vehicle. They had an oxygen mask on her in seconds, and someone was tugging on his hands.

"Sir, sir, let me see."

He'd nearly melted the skin off his face from his attempt to get inside. The fire demon consuming what was left of Shakedown would have had to bring more than that to have stopped him. It could have melted his bones down to ash—

he'd still have gone in for her.

"Luna," he rasped out. She blinked red-rimmed eyes up at him and reached her hand out for him.

A loud crack sounded, and a male voice shouted to *get back*. He turned just in time to see flames climb the sky thirty feet out of the back of the building, and the last of the roof collapsed in a fiery crackle.

Shakedown was gone.

32

———

Another fucking hospital. Carragh hated the smell, the squeaks of shoes on floors, the incessant sniffling and beeps. Worse, he hated knowing Luna was asleep in a room down the hall. She shouldn't be here at all.

After making sure she slept soundly with Sean watching over her, he strode to a different room—Declan's. His throat still burned, he had minor burns on his face, and his left hand was numb and engulfed in bandages, but fuck it. His right hurt like a son of a bitch, but it was at least relatively free with just three striped bandages over the worst of the burns. He wouldn't let them do more.

He rapped on the doorframe of the door with his knuckles.

Phee shot to her feet upon seeing him. "No." Her voice was emphatic, protective.

"I simply came by to see how he is." Man, his voice rasped.

Declan's head fell to the side on the pillow. Red-rimmed eyes stared at him out of a face that was red as if sunburned and glossy with some ointment smeared on it. Jesus, the man looked terrible.

"What can I do?" It was such an impotent offer, but he to at least make it.

"Do? You have done enough and…" Her words stopped when Declan's hand dropped over hers. She immediately put her attention back on him. He recognized the love that crossed between them. Is that what people saw when they saw him and Luna?

Declan, his hand as red as his face, gestured for him to come closer.

He did. "I had nothing to do with your club burning down, Declan." The words scratched like sandpaper, but they had to be said.

"I know." The man could barely get words out—they were mixed with gravel.

"That's a switch."

"But someone did." Someone torched that club on purpose—and he knew who.

Phee still glared at him, but a pissed-off woman he could handle. The fact his recent actions might have spurred on the fire? He'd spend his life making up for that fact.

Carragh took another burning breath. "The firemen said you went back in. For Luna? Anyone else? No one got…" How do you ask if anyone died?

"Everyone got out. Except…" Declan coughed. "Had to get something." The man raised his other hand and pointed at a canvas bag on a chair in the corner.

"Nothing is that valuable."

Declan lifted his eyes to him. "Those are." He gestured, and Phee seemed to understand. She brought the bag to him. "I have copies, but these… Originals. My mother's diaries."

Carragh shook his head in confusion. Given what he'd just gone through, the man shouldn't be talking, let alone worrying about some stupid diaries. There was sentimentality, and then there was stupidity.

Declan coughed. "The girls… need… go somewhere."

Phee hushed him. "Nathan already has Starr halfway… somewhere." She eyed Carragh. Good woman not to reveal locations.

He nodded once in the direction of her glare. It just seemed fitting to acknowledge her during this bizarre exchange.

"Go," Declan mouthed to Phee.

"I'm staying. No more discussion about it, either." Phee sat down next to Declan, and he gave her a weak smile.

Declan peered back up at him. "Luna."

"I've got her."

"No, you don't." Phee rose but then stilled when Declan touched her arm. Another unspoken message crossed between them.

Carragh stared deep into Phee's eyes—the blue so familiar yet so different. Residual pain floated there. Luna had said she took the brunt of their father's abuse.

"I'll cut out anyone's heart who dares to harm your sister, Miss O'Malley." He figured he couldn't go wrong with the formality.

"I'll hold you to that," she said tersely.

With some effort, Declan picked up the bag holding the journals. The man was clearly exhausted. "Read them. The blue one with the daffodil on it. Ten pages in." He began coughing so hard, Carragh wasn't sure he wouldn't hack up a lung.

Declan's hand fell to Carragh's wrist. Okay, he seemed desperate enough to touch him, so Carragh nodded once and took the bag. He knew of these legendary diaries. Declan had once used them as blackmail to get his father to ease off. Carragh thought Declan was crazy to expect such an impact on Tomas. Still did.

"It's not all," he managed to rasp out. So, there were more

things—things Declan may never share. He gained a truck-load of respect for the man in that second. Declan had kept something for himself—leverage. The man was smart and perhaps a MacKenna after all. They specialized in leverage.

Carragh nodded an acknowledgment. It suddenly felt important that Declan didn't hate him. Or maybe it was because the man had integrity—and belief that something like the scribblings of a woman dead long ago held such meaning. They were things Carragh wished he had.

Since he wasn't about to leave Luna—let a team of order-lies try to throw him out—he returned to her room with the canvas bag and sat himself down for a long night.

He adjusted the sheet so it was higher up on her body. She squirmed a little, her cheek falling to the side. An angry red slash marred her skin, and her complexion was ruddy yet ashen at the same time.

God, she was beautiful still.

He brushed a fingertip over her forehead. She didn't stir. The sedative they gave her must be strong as she didn't rise to waking.

His foot got tangled in the canvas bag he'd abandoned on the ground. So, his Aunt Kate had kept journals. For the life of him, he couldn't understand why it was so important to read the musings of a young pregnant woman hell-bent on leaving her family behind. He understood why she might, however.

After shuffling through the ten or so books, some a faded Moleskine, some with fancy patterns on them, he found the one Declan had referenced—a bright yellow daffodil adorned the front of a faded blue diary. The cardboard cracked a little as he opened it. Ten pages in, huh? He found it and began to read.

When the first page was read, he looked up at Luna, just needing to see something good for a minute. Because what was on the page? He thought he knew his father. He hadn't. Declan had been right about the records.

He returned to reading and didn't stop until he'd read every word written in a young woman's hand.

As he closed the last book, he stared at the woman he knew he'd spend the rest of his life with. Sending her to the Eastern Shore house wouldn't be enough. He couldn't send her without him, and he wasn't about to leave now. Not when he finally had what he needed.

He drew out his cell phone. He had some calls to make—including one that would likely end his father's reign for good.

33

Carragh stared down at his father, asleep. "My, how the mighty fall," he muttered. And so easily, too.

His father was a large man but was nearly incapacitated by something as microscopic as a razor-thin blood vessel bursting in his brain. Before he could philosophize too hard on that thought, Sean rapped on the door frame.

"Thought I heard you come in."

"What are you doing here?"

"Someone had to be." He gripped a coffee cup.

He didn't have time to play this game with Sean. "Was he awake when you got here?"

"He was."

"And?"

He shrugged. "And nothing."

A rasp came from his father's throat. Carragh tipped his head to view his father's lips moving as if trying to speak. His eyes blinked with more clarity after a moment.

"Carragh." The voice was weak, but it was there.

"Hello, Father. Having a nice day?" Carragh tapped the little blue diary against his leg.

Sean grumbled something behind him and stepped deeper into the room. As if he could stop his next actions? The man had no idea what was coming.

Carragh dropped into the chair behind him, slipped his finger in between the pages, and opened to the page he wanted. "Thought I'd come by and read to you." His eyes dropped down to the page. "*1970. May. The house is so quiet. Mother is crying in her room. Connor's funeral was so hard. I counted the petals on the flowers of every bouquet I could see, all placed around his casket. I couldn't go up to it, though. Why do people do open caskets? I was too scared that if I went up there he'd open his eyes. He'd then see I know how we got there.*"

Tomas' brow wrinkled. Sean stood like stone.

Carragh continued. "*I saw Tomas. There, I wrote his name and still my hand shakes. Tomas hit him with the boat paddle. He held his foot down on the man's face, and all that horrible gurgling? I can't stop hearing it. Things are getting worse. How do I get out of this wretched family? My brother drowned a man tonight. He drowned his best friend. Why won't Father believe me? Tomas scares me because I think this might just be the beginning.*" Carragh lifted his eyes from the page. "There's more, but I think you got the gist."

"What the hell is this, man?" Sean just shook his head.

"Kate MacKenna's diary." He held it up and inspected the spine in the harsh bedroom table lamp. "There are so many more, too. Father, you have quite the serial killer past."

"Carragh." Sean's warning tone really annoyed. "A girl's diaries? How do you know they are even true?"

Tomas laughed a little and then choked. He stared at Carragh. "Stupid little Kate. So what if she wrote some dreck? Like that means anything?"

"Oh, I'd say it'll mean a great deal to a great number of people in this town. Like Patrick—"

"You don't have the balls. Years ago bullshit. No one

cares." His words weren't articulated, but the man was putting up a bit of a fight. Let him.

Carragh wasn't in the mood for small talk. "Your rule over this family is over."

"Hardly."

He stood. "It's over. I came to give you fair warning." He lifted the diary. "I keep these to myself and everything that's in it. But you will turn over this family to me. That's the price."

"No." He glanced down at the diary Carragh still clutched. He laughed a little. "I never thought you'd be the soft one in the end. Daniel, I could see, but you?"

"I know letting go is hard, but you will one way or the other." Enough of his mad power declarations. He wasn't reacting anymore. "Like you said, family is everything. Protecting it. Too bad they were empty words to you. They aren't to me. So here is how it's going to go. We are divesting all holdings in Baltimore, Philadelphia, and New York."

Tomas coughed soundly. Carragh wasn't a monster, so he let the man finish his fit.

"Carragh, what the fuck are you doing?" Sean growled low. "What are you talking about?"

"I'm directing everything from now on. After all, Father, you're incapacitated."

His father's face reddened and his mouth didn't seem to want to work very well.

"Don't strain yourself. Take your time recovering. I've got things covered here."

Tomas stilled, his lips thinned. "So, my own son is my greatest threat now," he managed to grit out.

"Oh, but I am an enemy to anyone who opposes me. You taught me that much."

His father couldn't have expected to raise a viper and not

expect it to strike. Guess the man never counted on his fangs to sink into his own jugular vein.

Carragh turned away, unable to look at the man he shared his genes with.

Sean grasped his arm and hissed, "I repeat: what are you doing?"

"Freeing us."

"Us?"

He nodded once.

His father struggled to get up. "I knew you didn't love her."

That got him to turn around.

A sinister chuckle came out of his father. "You are so pussy whipped. You think making me your enemy is going to protect that little slut?" His eyes glanced Sean's way. "Afraid to do the wet work yourself? I'll take care of it then. You'll fold the second she's lying in the morgue."

"You won't touch her. You'd never survive in jail."

A roll of laughter as unsettling as unexpected thunder came out of Tomas. "You used to be a thinker, Carragh. If you know everything I've done, why do you think I'd stop now? One way ticket to hell… who cares? I'll kill her with my bare hands—just like I should have done to Kate the second she spread her legs for that boy. He was easy to sink in the ground, just like your little Luna—"

"You won't touch her or anyone else ever again." Carragh had ahold of his father's throat in a second and the man seized instantly, gasping and his eyes bulging.

Sean was on his back, yanking at his arms. "Let him go. Fuck, man…"

Carragh released his choke hold and shrugged off Sean. Tomas fell to his side, clutching at his throat, but then his lips curved into a satisfied smile. "There he is. My boy."

"You should rest. You're not well." Not any part of the man was.

"I'll do it. I'll do it." Tomas' choked tittering got louder as Carragh stomped out of the room.

His father had threatened to burn down Shakedown, so surely the torch job was under his orders. He sought to kill the woman he loved yesterday, and since it failed, his father would see it through.

Over Carragh's dead body.

Sean was on him in the hallway in a second. "What in the ever-lovin' shit is this?"

"You said you'd follow, right? Well, no more talk, Sean. Not now."

Sean's lips clamped shut and his stance widened. He wasn't happy at all—but his happiness wasn't high on Carragh's to-do list.

"What do you think you're doing?" The man's voice was pure gravel from a lifetime of smoking and age.

"I see you got my text." Carragh didn't bother to say hello either when he answered the call. In fact, he'd stopped with small talk altogether as the calls and texts streamed in as a response to his dozen or so messages to the other families in town.

All it took to dethrone his father was a few well-placed calls followed up by texted pictures of certain diary entries to some of the other Baltimore families. Wheels were in motion now that he couldn't stop if he wanted to.

Cracks in the tenuous loyalty people had to his father had formed—and they were growing with each passing hour as calls started coming in asking for more information, details, questions about rumors that reached their ears.

Carragh answered everyone succinctly and with no ambivalence. Yes, his father was guilty of the crimes outlined by his sister so long ago.

"I'm setting a rumor straight. It's all true, George. My father drowned your brother." Fifty years ago, Carragh's father and the man's son were best friends—at least until Tomas' legendary temper got the better of him. "What you do with this information is up to you. But know I'm taking over the family businesses and divesting it all. The MacKenna family will no longer want anything to do with whatever my father set up with you. It's all yours. Lock, stock, and barrel."

"Payoff?"

"Not in the slightest. The West is yours. As for the information I shared, like I said, you do what you need to. Just leave me out of it."

"I have no beef with you, Carragh. But Tomas?"

"Has lived a long life."

A chuff on the other end of the phone. Carragh supposed he'd never heard a son offer up their father before. Cold-hearted? Yes. But the man had successfully destroyed enough lives too many times in the past.

The mysterious drowning of a son.

The disappearance of a distant cousin.

The sudden departure of women to the West Coast.

They all could be explained by the confessions of Tomas bragging to rivals or anyone he was trying to cow—boastful speeches caught by his sister who hovered nearby.

It was time for the hold Tomas MacKenna once had over anyone to end—and to make his threats wholly impotent.

He placed his phone face down on the small cricket table next to his chair. His door slammed open.

Sean burst in and didn't knock. "What are you doing now?"

"Sean. Nice of you to drop by." He linked his fingers over his stomach.

"Are you crazy?" he scrubbed his hair. "Your father is flat on his back in his bed and you draw a target on him?"

"I see the rumors have gone around already." He hadn't expected them to fly so fast.

"Old Markson called me. Wanted to know if it was true."

"Ah, his daughter. God rest her soul."

Sean's nostrils flared. "It was thirty years ago. Different times."

"Didn't know rape and murder was okay back then, either." His phone buzzed as if on cue. He lifted it to see the name displayed on the screen. It was another distant family member calling about his text regarding their relative. That one was a car accident if memory served. Tomas always did for the dramatic.

The man raised his hand. "Not this way, Carragh. This is not the way to—"

"To what?" He leaned back in his chair. "What is it you think I'm doing?"

"You want to head this family—"

"I already do."

"And I suppose the stripper lying in your bed upstairs—" The man wisely stopped when Carragh shot to his feet. He always would have a bodily reaction to anyone disparaging her, wouldn't he? He didn't mind.

And hell yes, he had her upstairs. Drove her straight here this morning after her overnight hospital stay. He may never be separated from her again.

"Go ahead. Finish the sentence and see if I really am different from my father."

The guy's jaw muscles glided under his five o'clock shadow. His eyes drifted down to his phone, which dinged with yet another return text message.

"You're making a mistake." He shook his head. "For a burlesque club."

"Which someone burned down last night. I don't suppose you know anything about that?" He focused on his cousin's right hand—his greatest tell. It was the one where he jangled keys, twitched his fingers whenever he was trying to hide something. Tonight, they hung still by his side.

"It wasn't me if that's what you're asking."

"Good."

"I suppose now you're going to tell me you're marrying Luna."

My, his cousin really had let his imagination run away with him. "I'm sending Luna to—

"The Eastern shore?"

The man was fishing. Whatever. "Maybe."

Sean scrubbed his chin. "You think it's a good idea to leave now that you've ripped open every secret this family has?"

"Oh, it's not every one. And I'm not going anywhere." Leaving now was out of the question, but he had to get Luna somewhere no one from his circles knew the location of. Petra could drive her because he knew the man remained loyal despite the seeds planted by Sean.

Sean, however, was a different matter—and someone he'd deal with later.

"I've got to get this call, so later, Sean. That is if you still want to hang around."

He lifted his chin, his eyes drooping in fatigue. "You know I'm here for you," he said quietly—begrudgingly. Then he clumped out of the room. At least he shut the door quieter than when he arrived.

Carragh dropped back to the chair and lifted the phone. The night was young. And, for now, he had a few more things to say.

"Declan," he said into the phone. "Thanks for calling me back. I have news you're going to want to hear." He then gave Declan the assurance he would need to put the final puzzle piece in place. He'd deliver the backup information to prove what he said later.

The clock struck midnight before he got to his bed—where he joined a sleeping Luna Belle. As he slipped between the sheets, she rolled toward him.

She was still half-asleep, her eyes closed, her face nestled in his neck. *I love you, I love you, I love you*—Luna's hushed, raspy whispers crowded his brain. She'd inhaled so much smoke. Jesus, she'd almost died.

He punched down the wrath that rose in his chest, and ran his hand down her back. Under his fingers, her skin glowed in the twilight.

"Everything okay?" Her throat was too raw to be talking.

"You should be asleep, but yes, it's going to be. Rest your voice, love."

"Are you sure?" She slid her face back, her blue eyes shining in the dark. "If anything happened to you..." Her small hand fell to his cheek.

This woman. Of all the things to be worried about, his safety shouldn't be one of them.

He brought her hand to his lips and kissed the palm of her hand. "I love you, Luna Belle O'Malley." There wasn't anything else to say.

"Love you more," she smiled.

"Not possible." He rolled to his back, took her with him, and sighed. He would lie like this with her every night if it was the last thing he would do. It then dawned on him. It was possible if he'd just crash through that final barrier standing in their way.

His mind wasn't ready for sleep.

Her finger traced one of the dragon wings inked on his chest. "I love this. When did you get it done?" She did seem to have a fascination with it.

"Eighteen. Took a full year."

"Why a dragon?"

"To remind me to have courage."

"You knew even then this day would come?"

"Yes." Oddly, he had known—from age fourteen on. He may not have known exactly how his mother died, but he knew who was responsible. The man he was taking down —soon.

Her fingers fanned out, spanning the full inked wing. "Dragons are so misunderstood, especially in the movies." She lifted her head. "They are powerful and benevolent. They're protectors. At least that's what I believe." Her warm pink lips met the dragon head. "It suits you."

They say belief is powerful, but to have someone believe in you? *Liberating*.

He eased her away from him, rolled to his side and sat up. She joined him, the sheet slipping to reveal she was in one of his t-shirts. Nothing could look better on her.

"I want one, too." She pointed her finger at her heart. "Right here."

He captured her face with both hands. "Then you will have one."

Her lips stretched into a smile.

She would have everything she wanted because they were going to be together forever. Sean also had one good idea tonight, one Carragh was adopting sooner than later. "Luna Belle, marry me."

35

Luna sucked in a long breath and yanked open the door to the Phoenix Rising Dance Studio. The charred scent of burned wood still hung in the air like an unwanted guest. It didn't dissipate as she drew deeper inside.

Phee's studio was damaged in the Shakedown fire, a sight she couldn't even look at without her stomach turning over. Declan swore he'd fix Phee's studio, and they all believed him. Until then, it remained closed. And they were all out of a job for a while.

Deep murmurs sounded down the hall. When she entered the largest ballroom, Starr sat on the floor with Nathan, his ear pressed to her growing belly. She was smoothing down his hair and smiling down at him.

Phee and Declan stood talking off to the side. She hadn't expected to see Declan. His lungs were still burned from the fire, and her own throat still caught now and then.

Cherry was nowhere to be found. She was always late. It didn't matter. She knew more than most in this room about what Luna was going to have to tell them and what it would mean.

Starr sent her a wide smile upon seeing her.

"Hey, sorry I'm late." She'd needed a few minutes in the parking lot to steel her nerves. "Hi, Declan. I didn't expect you."

"Wouldn't miss it," he rasped.

"So, what's up?" Phee wrinkled her nose. "The workmen are starting soon, thank God. The smell in here is awful."

"That's fast."

"The sooner we put all this behind us, the better."

Yes, it was. She only hoped she wasn't about to pile on more damage.

Phee kissed her on her cheek. "You're not announcing *your* retirement, are you?"

Declan circled her sister's waist. "Let's hope not. I've already lost one great dancer."

"But gained a roommate, and you should rest your voice."

"Oh, more than that." He pressed a kiss to her neck.

So much love shone between them, her throat squeezed a little. Her sisters had found something good and true. Luna prayed they'd see that she had, too—even more than she thought possible in the unlikeliest place.

"Not retiring. I wouldn't do that to Declan. Remember that because I have other news."

"You and Max—"

"No." She shook her head adamantly and cleared her throat. "It's not Max. It's…" How could she do this? This was going to hurt them. Badly. They were never going to believe what she had to say—that she meant the words swimming on her tongue just dying to be spoken.

Declan's eyes softened. "Go on, Luna." He already knew what she was going to reveal, or at least part of it, didn't he? She could see her own truth reflected in his eyes. Carragh had said he and Declan had come to some understanding. Perhaps it was about her.

In fact, maybe she should have brought Carragh with her. She'd insisted she be alone to tell them. She didn't want him to have to hear their response.

Courage, she needed to display courage. "Carragh is taking his father down."

"Yeah, right," Phee scoffed. "He's a MacKenna."

"He can't help that. Just like we can't help our last names," Luna said.

Starr stepped forward, her face a still mask. "You're in love with him."

"She's been in love with him." Cherry's voice carried over her bootheel clicks. She dropped her huge bag at her feet. "Go on, baby girl. Tell them."

Phee cocked her head in accusation Cherry's way but then turned her glare to Luna.

Luna twisted her fingers. "Yes. I am."

Starr's mouth fell agape. "You can't be."

Phee closed her eyes and swallowed. A single tear escaped down her cheek. Luna grasped her sister's hand. "He's not like them."

That got her to open her eyes. So much fear. It nearly cracked her heart in two. "I promise you—"

"What? He's now going to replace his father?"

"He is," Declan said.

Nathan, who'd been quiet until that point, stood up and put Starr behind him. "Declan." His voice was pure ice.

Phee spun. "You knew?"

"I only knew about Carragh's plans but not about Luna. Just suspicions. And Nathan…" he looked up at the man. "Ruark is never getting out, and Tomas is going down for good."

Nathan just shook his head, his jaw a block of tension.

"Have I ever lied to you?" he asked the man. Then he looked down at Phee. "Have I?"

"Declan, please..." It wasn't like Phee to beg, but there it was.

He captured her chin in one hand. "Do you think I'd do anything to jeopardize you or anyone else here?" He glanced around the room. "I have something on Carragh. Handed to me by the man himself last night. Two jobs he was forced to do for his father."

"So?" Phee's watery eyes remain fixed on him.

"He handed me hard evidence. Files. Emails. Pictures. All of it."

"That just means he'll come after you more. It's a set-up."

"No, it's not." Luna stepped forward. "I don't know what he gave you, Declan, but..." she faced an ashen Starr, red-faced Nathan, and smug-looking Cherry. "He intervened on our behalf three times now. Once with you..." she nodded toward Starr and Nathan.

She then turned to Phee. "And again with you and Declan. And now? I'm with him. I love him." Her last words were tight, forced through a throat that wanted to burst with an odd combination of happiness and intense sorrow. If her sisters didn't accept him...

"I love him. I love him." The tears came. She couldn't stop them.

Phee pulled her into a hug. A few seconds later, Starr joined her. "I hope you know what you're doing, L.," Starr said into her hair. "Because I'll pluck every one of his gorgeous black hairs out of his head if there is one more tear shed because of that family."

That shook a slight laugh out of Phee, and Luna followed with a big sniff. Phee released them and stared at her sisters' faces. "I'll do it for you."

Cherry sidled up to them. "I'll help. We'll start with the hair on his balls."

That even got a half-smile out of Nathan but drew a

hearty laugh from Declan, which is all it took for her tears to stop.

"Thank you." Luna swiped under her eyes. "But no one touches his balls but me."

"Ewwww." Starr raised her hand, which Luna grasped.

Everyone stilled once more.

"And I have to tell you something else. Just remember. Sisters forever. Friends always." She gazed at Starr, who nodded slowly. She then turned to Phee, who gave her a tighter nod.

Okay, deep breath. "We drove to Virginia and got married this morning."

36

Carragh swiveled the chair and studied the painting over the credenza in his father's office, not quite visible in the dark. But then he knew it by heart, having stood on the other side of his father's desk, waiting for the man to turn the fuck around. He liked making people wait. That little habit would prove useful tonight.

The silence in the house finally broke. It started with the front door opening and Petra greeting the visitors. Then the click of high heels—not the delicate tap of Luna's steps but the harder clacks of Nicole's. Sean's shoe scuffs accompanied her, just as he suspected. It was easy to tell it was him by the keys jangling by his hip.

At the office door, Petra's voice. "He's in the study. Waiting."

"Glad to see you're keeping an eye out," Sean said.

"I've always been loyal. Sir."

Sean wouldn't have caught the tightness in Petra's voice. His cousin never was a detail guy, but Carragh knew the man was barely holding back his temper given what he'd shared with him—Sean's suspicions about the man's loyalty and now Carragh's own suspicions about his cousin.

Carragh flipped his father's lighter back and forth a few times as they entered. Light from the hallway spilled in.

"Sir?" Sean called.

"Speak." He slurred his words on purpose. "No light." Just in case they got any bright ideas.

"Sorry, I lost 'em, but I won't let you down. I'll take care of her."

"The sooner the better, Sean." Nicole's haughty tone made Carragh tighten his grip on the lighter. "Jesus. If you don't get rid of her, I will. I have no qualms about dropping her body on what's left of Holland Island."

Sean chuffed. "Like your work at Shakedown. You'd have loved it, sir. Place went up like a box of matches. Nicole's quite the pyro." He chuckled and a female voice joined him.

"What can I say? Flame is my signature color."

A beat of silence. He would see them hang themselves fully.

Sean widened his stance. He didn't even need to see the move to know the sounds of a man seeking better footing—and probably more compliments for his good soldier antics.

"But Carragh—"

"Always playing the white knight," Nicole interrupted. The slide of fur against the chair before the desk sounded. So, Nicole was making herself at home.

"Yeah… he is going to be a problem. So, if you need me to pull the trigger… I mean, whatever you say."

"You can't wait for me," Nicole tittered. "The man has proven untamable. He'd prefer the fire crotch."

Sean joined her laughter. "Maybe she'll light his dick on fire."

Carragh had heard enough. "Oh, she does more than that." He turned the chair to face them. "Petra. Light, please."

The man understood and switched on the table lamp. Sean could have taken a lesson or two on stealthiness. Even Carragh hadn't heard him slink in behind them.

Nicole shot to standing. "Carragh."

Sean tensed, his hand moving to his hip.

"Oh, I wouldn't do that… cousin."

Petra's gun was at the back of Sean's head in seconds. Perhaps Sean would learn. The devil *is* in the details—like how Petra was once his bodyguard, and skills like his were rarely lost in age.

Both of Sean's hands shot into the air. "Whoa, now. I don't know what you think…"

Nicole had the smarts to at least show fear. "I had nothing to do with any of this. Your father said to. Ordered it, actually." She was backing up.

Carragh rose. "Sit down, Nicole. As for you, Sean, I knew you could lie. It wasn't Petra at all. It was you all along. The two of you."

Behind Petra, more delicate heel clicks sounded. Luna rounded him and scooted closer to Carragh. He pulled her behind him just in case Sean was not only disloyal but stupid as fuck and tried to make a move.

"What the fuck is that stripper doing here?" Nicole gritted out.

Carragh's gaze shot to the woman. "You treat my wife with respect."

Sean's face dropped. "Your…"

"Wife. We were married this morning."

Luna's hand tightened on his.

"Ah, nothing warms the heart like a family meeting." Patrick Monroe's loud voice sounded in the doorway. He stepped just inside. "Nicole."

Her nostrils flared like a horse. "Daddy?"

"Quiet."

"This is just a misunderstanding." A nervous laugh.

"Yes. You thought you could operate alone. Silly girl." He wasn't smiling. "You better keep your word better than your father, Carragh."

Sean's hand was on his pistol. "Stand down, Sean. Now, listen up… all of you. I have enough blackmail material to send you all down."

Patrick's jaw tensed.

Sean, however, couldn't leave well enough alone. "Now listen—"

"Shut up, Sean. Patrick and I have come to an understanding." A big one. It was simple really.

The Kate MacKenna diaries, hidden by Declan for years, had proven useful. He shook enough people out of the woodwork the last few days who didn't like seeing their loved ones' names splashed in a young girl's diaries—next to how his father gutted them.

His father was now persona non grata with the other families in town. Patrick wanted his deals to go through—he'd have to do so without the MacKenna backing. To sweeten the pot? He couldn't wait to see Sean's face with this next bit of news.

"I'm out of my father's business. Patrick can have all the contacts and dealers my father ever did business with. I'll stay out of his business and he'll stay out of mine. Our product lines don't mix. I don't care about his—"

"And I could give a shit about energy. What a crock," Patrick sneered.

"Your father—" Sean started.

"Is incapacitated and therefore I have taken over. It's a done deal. Paperwork and everything. Imagine that." He let a smirk spread across his face.

Of course, several people now wanted his father dead, but he supposed the man had dug his own grave. He'd protected him by also spreading the word he was wheelchair-bound and Carragh had him under strict surveillance. Anyone dared to do anything—to his father, him, or anyone he cared about—then the arrangements he'd made would go into motion. Tomas' meticulous paperwork on his dealings with them would be released to the media, public officials, the FBI, and the Justice Department.

It wasn't the 1920s anymore—they may have had finesse in their killings but they didn't have what today's families had: a love for money and business that transcended the need for pure revenge. It would just be easier to let them all live.

Nicole's irritating voice cut his way. "You are a fool, Carragh MacKenna. Go on, fuck your slut—"

"Nicole, come on." Patrick grabbed ahold of Nicole's arm. "Before I have to leash you."

"But—"

"Now." He jerked his head toward the doorway.

It was a good thing he yanked her out of there because Carragh didn't trust himself with the woman.

Sean scratched the side of his chin, stared down at the floor, and let out a half-laugh. "Jesus, Carragh." He raised his face and sliced his eyes toward Luna, who remained next to him. "For that." He lifted his chin her way.

He didn't have any more patience for the guy. "You are on probation."

"Probation? Fuck that, and fuck you."

"You showed loyalty to my father. Now you're going to swear it to me."

"And why would I do that?"

"We're family."

Luna slipped her hand into his. "Family matters."

Sean sneered anew. "What would you know about it?"

"She knows more than you do. Clearly. You want to go work for Patrick there, have at it."

Sean gave a tight shake of his head.

"Good. You swore allegiance to my father. Now you're going to swear it to me."

"You always had it."

"Except for that little part of about pulling the trigger?"

"Appeasing an old man."

"I'll tell you how you're going to appease me. You're going to rebuild Shakedown."

"What? Work for Declan Phillips?"

"Yes, actually. And pay for it. I don't care how long it takes to pay back."

The man's face fell, and after a long minute, he nodded once. It was enough—for now. The man would be watched—closely—for a while. Hell, maybe forever. But Carragh wasn't his father. He didn't put bullets in people who opposed him.

He also had too much to do to worry about petty revenge schemes because no one would get him out of the driver's seat now. Not ever.

37

Six Months Later - November

Carragh absent-mindedly stared at the small picture of a pheasant over the bureau. He growled and yanked the tie free from his neck for the third time.

Luna went to him and grasped his arm. "Here. Let me."

He twisted, and she went to work on knotting his tie. "You didn't need to get this dressed up. It's just my sisters."

"Exactly." He peered down at her. "And Declan. And Nathan. And Cherry."

The zing of silk through the tie knot made her belly tingle. She did love her man in a suit. "There." She patted his pecs. "Cherry didn't want to be left out. You'll learn that about her. She's part of our family, too." Not to mention she was the reason this night was happening at all.

"Oh, I get that." He reached over to the chair and grabbed his jacket. "I can't believe they all said yes."

"It's because they know past animosities are over." Or so she hoped. They would wait and see how tonight unfolded.

"You've more than proven yourself, Carragh. You don't need to any longer."

He murmured his disbelief.

"Seriously. They'll love you as I do in time."

"Let's hope not." He captured her around her waist and drew her flush against his torso, which was so unfair because he knew what being this close did to her. Her imagination needed no dinner or family time. It only desired him, preferably *out* of the suit and her dress abandoned on the floor.

"I have some special love reserved just for you." He tilted his pelvis so his impressive cock pressed into her stomach.

The man's testosterone levels had risen in recent months—and it hadn't been low before. Now, not a day went by the man didn't reach for her where it ended up with her clothes falling off.

The doorbell chime sounded downstairs, and her lips burst wide open. "They're here."

Carragh's return smile was slow coming, but it finally appeared. "Our first Sunday dinner. I had no idea you could cook for so many."

"Oh, just you wait."

They both went to the front door to greet their guests. Phee, Declan, and Cherry faced them, all wearing different moods. If Luna knew anything, it was how to read her family.

Phee was containing some disdain, and Declan's face was unreadable. Cherry seemed quite happy to be standing on the front porch of Luna and Carragh's new Roland Hills home, having just moved in a month ago.

"I love that," Cherry pointed at the double-wide porch swing Carragh had put up for Luna as a welcome present—one of many. "Oh, and such beautiful landscaping." Cherry did love her aesthetics.

"Welcome, and come in." Carragh stepped back and gestured them inside.

Once inside, Phee thrust a dish covered in tinfoil at her. "Here. Declan made biscuits." She reached over and gave Luna a half-hug. Her eyes then began to roam around the room.

Carragh collected coats. Fall had officially set in with chillier evenings. They'd spent a glorious summer living at Carragh's house. "Our house," he kept correcting her. She loved even thinking that phrase.

She hadn't been successful getting her sisters to visit, however, at least not until Cherry finally intervened. Cherry really should have gone into politics.

Carragh had had quite a busy summer unravelling decades of his father's work, but they'd still managed to have some getaways to the Eastern Shore house. Fixing it up a little was the next project on her to-do list—even if most of her weekends would soon be taken up again once Shakedown re-opened.

"I can't wait until summer comes around again when we can sit out on the porch and swing our troubles away," Luna said.

"Oh, and what troubles would that be?" Phee handed her forest green velvet jacket to Carragh. Despite her sarcastic tone, she wasn't too sorry to be here. Phee had worn her favorite jacket.

"We don't have those anymore." Luna smiled at her sister. "Remember?"

"We'll see."

Footsteps on the porch signaled Starr and Nathan had arrived, and they strode in through the open front door. "Fashionably late, but I have the best excuse. Little Phoebe here decided three a.m. was a perfect time to choreograph a new dance."

Starr was due in a month, and it showed given the size of her belly. It was huge, beautiful, and made Luna pine for the day she might get to feel a little being flutter and kick inside her.

"Forgive me for not bringing anything to dinner?" She glanced up at Carragh. "I figured you'd have enough." She waved her hand around the room. Nathan huffed a little as if amused.

Okay, rocky start, but they'd warm up. Surely, they wouldn't be this rude. It really wasn't like them.

"Come on in. We'll have drinks first."

"Wow, you sound like the matron of a grand estate already." Starr hooked her arm in Luna's.

"Nothing grand. Just us."

While Carragh poured drinks, he and Declan chatted amicably enough. Nathan remained silent, sitting next to Starr. He was uncomfortable by the way he kept his elbows on his knees, trying not to look at anything. *That* she'd expected.

Phee and Starr talked about babies and pretty much ignored everyone.

Cherry, however, acted as if she'd landed in heaven by the way she wandered the room, drinking in every art deco statue Carragh had on display.

"Why, Carragh, you have quite the eye." She bent over to more closely inspect the woman holding the peacock feather, nearly the size of her whole body.

"I knew you'd love that one." Luna joined her. "See all the detail?"

"Since when did you care about art?" Phee asked.

"I care about a lot of things."

"Things," she drew out.

Luna gave her a hard look. "Phee." She did not hide her

warning tone. Her sister needed to remove that large stick from her butt right now.

Her sister sighed and sipped her sparkling cider.

At dinner, things seemed to lighten up. Everyone chatted about current news, dance classes, and the new Shakedown club Declan and Carragh were building together—thanks to Carragh's over-the-top gesture of donating his warehouse space down the street. Apparently, he was making Sean foot much of the renovation bill, too. He'd been the one to suggest Nicole start the fire to begin with.

Luna suppressed a shudder that Nicole was still out there somewhere, an obsessive arsonist who wouldn't likely give up easily. Carragh said not to worry, that she had more things to worry about—like her father, who took her independence badly.

Carragh's hand fell to hers. "Everything alright?"

"I'm fine. Just happy everyone is here. In fact…" She rose her voice over the dining and light laughter around her and Carragh's table. *Their* table. What a thought. "Thank you, everyone, for being here. We haven't had a family dinner in too long."

Nathan choked a little and swallowed his filet. Starr slapped him on the back and handed him his water. "I'd say. Next time let's do it at our place. Less stress all around."

Luna couldn't see Starr's eyes as she was focused on Nathan, but she got her intent. Luna appreciated the protective sense Starr had. She had as well, just for a different man.

"We're in, Starr. We'd love that." Phee glanced at Declan and they shared a certain "look." Luna read it very well. It said, "We did our duty. We won't be doing it again."

Enough.

Luna clinked her glass and rose from her seat.

"Oh, yes, a toast." Cherry nearly bounced in her seat. She raised her wine glass.

"No toast. There hasn't been enough to celebrate… yet." She let her eyes drift around the room, taking in each member of her family. Her lips couldn't have formed a smile if she'd wanted them to.

She circled to behind Carragh and placed her hands on his shoulders. He stared up at her, brows furrowed in question.

"This is how it's going to go from this second forward," she said rather loudly. "Carragh is my husband. Forever. We are going to have a life together. I want that life to include all of you." She peered down at him, and he crossed his arm over his chest to lay his hand on hers.

She stared hard at Starr. "If you'd just stop judging, you'd discover how wonderful he is. Put everything on the line for us. And he's kind…" she looked over at Phoenix "…when other people aren't being kind."

Phee lifted her water goblet to her lips and sliced her eyes to the side, and Starr dropped her gaze down to her lap.

"And if you can't be, you know where the front door is."

Both of her sister's gaze lifted, their eyes widened. Luna had never laid down a line like this, one that would put them on the "outs." She meant it when she'd said 'Sisters forever, friends always,' but being a sister meant embracing the others' choices.

When Luna thought about it—*really* thought about it— her mistakes in the past weren't in just finding their father or not getting between her sisters and their father when he had his belt out, buckle on the striking end, and raised his arm to strike them. It was not *speaking up*.

Cherry delicately lifted a shrimp to her lips, but Luna caught her hidden smile.

"Does anyone have anything to say?" she asked.

Silence stretched for a long minute. She could wait.

"These shrimp are fantastic," Cherry whispered when the

silence grew too great for her to bear. Lightening things up wasn't what they needed right now, but she appreciated the effort.

"Okay, more needs to be said." Luna took in a long breath. "I'm sorry I don't have as many scars as you on my body. I'm sorry I forced a reunion with dad. But I'm not sorry about loving the most wonderful, strongest man I've ever known." Carragh twisted his neck so he could lay a kiss on her fingers.

"We were going to be better than Dad. Now you can prove it."

Phee swallowed, probably trying to stem the tears brimming in her eyes. Starr blinked and took a long breath.

It was time to end this animosity for good. She lifted her glass. "So, here's my toast. Family forever. Friends always."

Phee smiled, a single tear falling to her cheek. She slapped at it.

Starr took a long look at her but then lifted her glass. "I like that." She tried to push her chair back as if she wanted to rise. She struggled so much Nathan jumped up and pulled her chair out. As he did, his eyes met Luna's for one brief second, and he dipped his chin in a single nod.

He wasn't much of a talker, but she got his message. Luna's own eyes began to fill. If Nathan could call up any forgiveness for the last year, everyone else could.

Slowly, one by one, everyone else rose from their chairs, glasses in hand. Carragh was the last one to stand. He pushed his chair back to make room for her so she could stand next to him.

He lifted his glass high. "Family forever."

Nathan reached around Starr and grabbed a water glass. He lifted it toward Carragh.

Oh, yes, this was going to work.

Glasses raised high, Luna finished the toast. "Friends always."

"Amen," Starr and Phee said in unison.

Like a deflated hot air balloon, all the tension in the room fell to the ground. All around the table, hands had clenched glasses and faces had been strung tight, but any strings the past held on them somehow loosened. Foreheads relaxed and smiles were let loose.

"Hear, hear," Cherry tapped her palm in a half clap. "Well, finally." She plopped herself down and everyone else took their seats again and snapped napkins back in place.

Cherry reached for the bowl of mashed potatoes. "Momma Cherry can finally get a good night's sleep because the O'Malley sisters are. In. Their. Love. Nests."

"And their husbands, too." Carragh winked at her.

Cherry dipped her chin down and to the side. "Oooo, Carragh MacKenna, methinks we might be kindred spirits after all." She half-rose and leaned over the table. She plopped a huge portion of potatoes on his plate. "Now. Eat. Then we all shift our discussion to the new show coming out of Shakedown. In time for a new Christmas-Hannukah-Kwanza holiday extravaganza. I hereby predict it."

"I should have never made her creative director," Declan chided.

"You're right. I should be…" she looked thoughtful "…Creative Vice President." She blocked the words in the air.

"It does have a ring to it." He clinked his glass against hers.

"Doesn't it, though? Just like Nathan and Starr Baldwin. Declan and Phoenix Phillips. And…" she pointed her glass at Luna "…Carragh and Luna MacKenna."

Glasses then rose into the air again, and the laughter came back. That's what Luna wanted around this table—

often. Laughter from her sisters, from their men, Cherry, her husband, and soon, Starr's baby.

Then someday? She reached for Carragh's hand again, and his blue eyes, now more fire than ice, cast all his love down on her. *Someday*, their baby's giggles would join the celebration.

38

———

February

His father's wheelchair bumped over the cracks in the walkway. When they got to the thirteenth marker, he pushed it down onto the grass. "Careful," his father grumbled. The man couldn't stop giving him orders.

Luna's hand slipped around his arm, and her reassuring fingers curled around his bicep. She gave him a sly smile as if she, too, had caught his father's tone. They were sharing more of those moments—little messages that only they could understand. Such a silly thing for him to notice, but it comforted him in a way.

He'd wanted to bring Luna to his mother's grave so many times over the last many months, but the timing had to be right. He wasn't yet sure about last year's bombshell actions—outing his father's past, divesting the family of his father's holdings. Turned out no one really cared in the end. Times had changed.

Perhaps it was because the MacKennas were now one less

player among the less-scrupulous masses. It was an easy thing to swallow in a fiercely competitive crime circuit.

Or perhaps it was because he so spectacularly sold off every building—save those on the waterfront near Shakedown—and shut down every supply chain he could identify. Instead, selling everything for pennies on the dollar to rivals, handing over every phone number and contacts he could drum up to them. He didn't need the money or the lines of business.

In fact, all he really cared about was standing next to him.

He turned the wheelchair to face the granite angel, his mother's grave marker. He got close. Let the man look upon at least one of the deaths he'd likely caused.

Luna stepped forward and set the bouquet of daffodils and white lilies she'd brought at the marker's base. "It's beautiful." She lifted her eyes to him.

"It's… adequate." Of all the times he'd stood here, his throat had never closed like this before. Maybe because he was entirely incapable of hiding anything in his wife's presence. *My wife.* Would he ever get used to that term, even in his own thoughts?

Her small hand slipped into his. "Introduce me to your mother?"

He scratched the side of his face, then pulled her closer. "Hello Mother. This is Luna Belle, my wife."

Her hand slipped free. "Hello Mrs. MacKenna. I'm Valentina."

"You don't usually use that name." He had known her real name for a while, just had never heard her utter it since their wedding ten months ago. It was as beautiful as her stage name.

She peered up at the angel. "I'm not ashamed of my real name. I just got used to my sisters calling me Luna. It helped with Phee, who definitely didn't want her real name out there." She smiled over at him. "Your mother would have understood that, I think."

She was right, of course. His mother would have loved Luna. *Valentina.*

"Mrs. MacKenna, I'm in love with your son. I'll take good care of him."

A murmur came from his father.

"What's that? Want to say something?" Carragh didn't hide his disdain.

Luna threw him a stern look. She'd softened to the guy. He hadn't. He made sure his father had nursing care around the clock, but his past wouldn't be forgiven easily. And certainly not while standing here.

"She'll do." Tomas jutted his chin up once. "She has respect."

Carragh muttered and swallowed the retort souring on his tongue. The man knew so little about respect.

"You mother…" His father fumbled his words. The man's speech had returned but he didn't talk much anymore. "I don't come because it reminds me. She took the bullet. Got in front of me. Took it for me." He pointed to his chest and then pointed at the angel.

Carragh's limbs filled with concrete. "What do you mean?"

Tomas' watery eyes gazed up at him. "You know."

His brain shut off for a second. That had to be the only reason why he couldn't think. His mother saved this man's life?

Luna was by him again in a second. He squeezed her hand and took a long breath.

"Who did it?" he gritted out.

"Why? Want to avenge her?" His father waved his hand. "Buried him long ago."

Shit. He scrubbed his forehead. Of course, his father had.

That was his way. Take down anyone who got in the way. But then his mother… got in the way. To save this man he now stared down at? Broken, moral-less, and beyond repair?

"No more burials." His chest was so tight it was hard to get out the words, but he had to. The killings had to stop. He thought he had ended his father's way of life—starting with the overthrow of the business. Would it ever be enough?

"Yes." His father managed to get out with some effort. "Family. Sacred." He thumped his chest with his fist.

The man's ego, just like his decline was unstoppable. In fact, he barely spoke anymore, but, Jesus, these were the words that came out of him today?

Carragh glanced up at the angel he'd stared at every Sunday for years—*fucking years.*

Luna suddenly knelt in the grass, her head bowed, and her lips moved as if in prayer.

His father harrumphed. "Yes, respect." As if he knew the definition of the concept?

Then the answer came so clearly. What would his mother want? She'd want Carragh to live, to love, to have a family of his own. That's all she'd ever wanted.

He turned to his father. He needed more from the man. There was one final piece of his future that only Tomas Mackenna could give him.

Carragh stared hard at his father. "Now you show some respect. Say it."

He chuffed. "Say what?"

Carragh stood there, waited. He'd been waiting his whole life for this day so what were a few more minutes?

His father clasped his hands together and stared down at the ground. He finally raised his heavy lids to him. "Be careful what you wish for."

"No more wishing."

Someone cleared his throat behind him. He'd heard the

footsteps and thought it might be Petra. When he turned, he faced Declan—and Phoenix, and Starr, who held her little baby girl.

He sucked in a long breath. *Huh. Back-up.* That's what this was—maybe just for Luna, but perhaps… Nah, it was a little early to dream of her sisters taking him in with open arms. For now, they treated him like a distant uncle. Cordially, and with a modicum of respect. It was enough for now.

Declan raised his chin. Phoenix's face was still, but at least she didn't glare at him, which was real progress.

Carragh had fulfilled his promise of rebuilding Shakedown even if he hadn't poured the gasoline and lit the match that took it down. Declan lost his precious antiques that he'd been selling off to keep the place going. Thank God for fire insurance, though how do you put a price on sentimentality?

After donating his warehouse down the street for the new club, he'd ordered Sean to work construction. The man wanted to be muscle, let him. It gave Carragh a smug satisfaction to know the man took to it—ordering workers about, looking contrite but oddly happy in a way.

Starr lifted her baby's arm and waved once. Baby Phoebe's face was as still as the angel's face on his mother's marker. Man, had he ever slept that soundly?

He glared down at his father once more, the man who'd been responsible for most of his sleepless nights. "You know what I want. My family."

His father sucked air between his teeth and let it out. "The family is yours."

Luna's profile showed a sly smile forming, though her eyes remained closed, her head bent. She made the sign of the cross.

Carragh inclined his head, then rounded to his father's side and placed his hand on the man's shoulder. It was more than he deserved, but being surrounded by people who once hated him but now were beginning to warm to his presence, a sliver of charity rose in his heart.

Luna pushed herself to standing and smiled at the crowd behind him. She then mouthed *I love you* to him. She joined him, slipped her hand in his, and they resumed their silent vigil in front of the angel.

Starr's little girl cooed in the background, and her hushed whispers to the child floated in the air. The wind picked up and blew some stray leaves around the concrete and granite markers lined up like mismatched soldiers. They should go but he couldn't make himself move.

He sent up a little prayer, thanking whoever looked down on them for letting him live to see this moment, to have won the heart of a good woman, to have finally claimed his own destiny—not the one handed down to him.

Someday, his life would be over. Someday, everyone around him would be like these deceased souls lying underground, too. But not for a while—he'd make sure of it.

His father would likely die of natural causes. The man didn't deserve it.

But Carragh would make sure that was how he was going to go out as well—and his children. Little boys and girls with eyes like Luna's, their mother's, as blue and free as an open sea.

EPILOGUE

"You know Cherry is going to be pissed she wasn't invited." Phee cocked her foot, stared at its reflection in the small mirror. A dozen show boxes lay open, tissue paper crinkled over the sides.

Any day that involved shoe shopping was a good day.

"I'm getting her those cowboy boots over there." Luna pointed at the turquoise special edition boots.

She then stood and teetered on the four-inch red sparkle heels. "And some things sisters need to do for themselves."

"Yeah, like talk each other into every pair they want. I can't wait until Nathan catches me in something that doesn't have baby spit on it." Starr groaned. "How do they look?" The soft pink sandals with little rosettes lining the straps were gorgeous.

"Like someone might call child protective services if you wear them holding Phoebe for fear of harming the baby."

She laughed at Phee's assessment. Funny how "child protective services" didn't elicit any bad feelings from them anymore.

"Okay, that settles it. I need them. And you need those red ones, L."

"Like I need a fourth pair of red? No, I'm getting the black with silver sequin straps. Classier."

"Well, la-di-da over there." Phee cocked her head. "Now that you live in Roland Park."

"We're thinking of moving." She lifted the heel to see its construction. She and Carragh had a fundraiser to attend that night for the Mental Wellness Association of Maryland.

"What?" Starr and Phee asked in unison.

"To one street over," she emphasized. "We need a bigger house."

Phee made a *pffft* sound. "Like that huge monstrosity isn't big enough already?"

Their new house wasn't that big. His father's home a street over was larger, not that she'd seen much of it. Her super-possessive husband refused to let her visit his father, who was under 24-hour nursing care now. Carragh had wanted to stay close. "To keep an eye on him," he'd said.

"Why on earth would you need something more to clean?" Starr rolled her eyes.

Luna put the top on the box of black sandals and rose. "We need room for the twins." She smiled at her sisters and patted her belly. "Nine weeks."

Loud squealing ensued, which nearly had her heart happily bursting its blood vessels. *Bingo.* Just the reaction she wanted.

"Keeping it from you has been killing me," she called into the fray.

Phee pulled her into a huge hug and Starr jumped up and down and clapped—which was amazing given she was still in the four-inch sandals.

Thank God they were excited. It hadn't been easy for them to accept Luna was Mrs. Carragh MacKenna. He'd offered for her to keep her maiden name as an olive branch. No way.

Carragh had turned the family around—or was almost there—and she'd wanted in on the action.

Every night at dinner, before she had to head to the new Shakedown for her one or two acts—she couldn't give up dancing just yet—he'd talk to her, fill her in on his day.

On her off nights, they often went to events and fundraisers, and sometimes back to that little speakeasy where he'd bared his soul to her that first time. He'd ask for her input, and she gave it. He didn't always take her ideas, but the fact he listened to her at all? She didn't think she could love him any more, but every day she did.

She was his person. And while no one would ever replace her sisters, he was hers.

Luna fingered her mother's locket, which she always kept on a long chain around her neck. No one should be completely forgotten. "So, I'm thinking you both could be godparents, like one for each."

Phee's eyes misted. "I'd love that." She and Declan would never have children by choice, but given the way she'd taken to all the babies she insisted everyone brought to her mothers-only dance classes, she'd make a wonderful godmother.

Starr huffed a happy breath. "Well, that does it. We're going to Bloom and Blossom Babies next."

Luna clasped her hands together. "I really had hoped you'd say that. Their winter collection came in—"

"You're on their speed dial aren't you?" Phee laughed.

"No. Maybe."

A pause filled the room as they stood there in a triangle, holding hands without even trying. Their hands just reached for each other. She was so lucky. She'd always had her sisters, and they had her. A niggling sadness threatened her happiness that Carragh didn't grow up with such champions—

only promised rewards if he did what he was told. Well, he had the O'Malley sisters as his backup now.

"Is it possible?" Phee whispered. She didn't even have to finish her question.

Starr smiled. "It's odd, isn't it? Like we've arrived or reached a place or…" Her eyes got dreamy in thought as if searching for the answer.

"We're home," Luna finished. "Family forever. Friends always."

"Amen," Starr and Luna said in unison.

They did go to Bloom and Blossoms next, and after Phee and Starr bought more clothes at the baby store—really, they put her to shame in the purchasing department—they parted to go to their respective men.

Starr's laughter filtered down the street as she hugged Phee one more time. Phee climbed into her vintage VW, and Starr tripped merrily to her car.

Luna paused for a second. Her heart didn't skip a beat at seeing them go three separate ways. How long had it been since that happened?

Phee waved as her car rumbled by, and Starr tooted her horn as she did a U-turn in the street to head in the opposite direction. Luna would see them tomorrow—and every day after that. There were dance classes to teach and attend. Shows to put on. Babies to love.

And they'd do it all together because no one on God's green earth could tear the O'Malley-now-Baldwin-Phillips-MacKenna sisters apart. Not ever again.

Oh, and Luna got that dragon tattoo—right over her heart.

Thank you for reading the Shakedown Series. I hope you enjoyed Luna and Carragh's journey. Missed the other

Shakedown books, Tough Luck or Tough Break? Access them from your favorite online retailer.

Visit ElizabethSaFleur.com to sign up for her email newsletter or just to browse. I have sooo much happening, book-wise, in the near future.

ALSO BY ELIZABETH SAFLEUR

Elite

Holiday Ties

Untouchable

Perfect

Riptide

Lucky

Fearless

Invincible

The White House Gets A Spanking

Spanking the Senator

Tough Road

Tough Luck

Tough Break

Tough Love

ABOUT THE AUTHOR

Elizabeth SaFleur writes romance that dares to "go there" from 28 wildlife-filled acres, dances in her spare time and is a certifiable tea snob.

Find out more about Elizabeth on her web site at www.ElizabethSaFleur or join her private Facebook group, Elizabeth's Playroom.

Follow her on Instagram (@ElizabethLoveStory) and TikTok (@ElizabethSaFleurAuthor), too!